INNOCENT
HEROES

TUNDRA BOOKS

INNOCENT HEROES

Stories of Animals in the First World War

SIGMUND BROUWER

Tundra Books, a division of Random House of Canada Limited,
a Penguin Random House Company

Library and Archives Canada Cataloguing in Publication

Brouwer, Sigmund, 1959–, author
Innocent heroes / Sigmund Brouwer.

Issued in print and electronic formats.
ISBN 978-1-10191-846-3 (hardback).—ISBN 978-1-10191-847-0 (epub)

1. Animals—War use—Juvenile fiction. 2. Animals—War use—Anecdotes—Juvenile literature.
3. World War, 1914–1918—Canada—Juvenile fiction. 4. World War, 1914–1918—Canada—
Juvenile literature. 5. Human-animal relationships—Juvenile fiction. 6. Human-animal
relationships—Anecdotes—Juvenile literature. I. Title.

PS8553.R68467I66 2017   jC813'.54   C2016-900967-X
                                                   C2016-900968-8

Published simultaneously in the United States of America by Tundra Books of Northern New York,
a division of Random House of Canada Limited, a Penguin Random House Company

Library of Congress Control Number: 2016933014

Edited by Samantha Swenson

Designed by Leah Springate
Printed and bound in the United States of America

Jacket and chapter opener images (poster) *Your Chums Are Fighting—Why Aren't You?*
Source: Library and Archives Canada/National Archives of Canada fonds/c029484k;
(barbed wire) © Kelpfish | Dreamstime.com; (dog silhouette) © Art-Y / Getty Images;
(vintage card) © Davor Ratkovic | Dreamstime.com

www.penguinrandomhouse.ca

1   2   3   4   5   21   20   19   18   17

TUNDRA BOOKS | Penguin Random House

DEDICATION

Much gratitude to the Horizon School Division in Saskatchewan for support of this project—and especially to Kevin Garinger, Director of Education, and Katherine Oviatt, Supervisor of Literacy and Learning Services, who made it possible to spend so much time with the 2015–2016 ELA Grade 9 students at Punnichy High School for ongoing advice, discussions, questions and comments about Thomas Northstar's role in the platoon's fictional narrative. To teacher Kelly Schermann and the students at Punnichy High School, I share your dream that some day it will truly be one blood and one nation.

This book is dedicated to:

Kathy Oviatt

Kelly Schermann

Joe Bear

Raven Bigsky

Mercedes Bigsky-McKay

Jayden Bitternose

Kendall Bitternose

Dennis Bruce

Ty Bull

April Desjarlais

Sydney Desjarlais

Hyson Dubois

Wyatt Dubois

Brian Fisher

Maddy Gordon

Cassidy Grey

Tia Hunter

Lennae Kinequon

Demetrius McNab

Elias McNab

Angel Morin

Garret Pelletier

Tianna Pelletier

Tiara Pelletier

Tiara Pratt-McNabb

Chad Runns

Spencer Taypotat

Aaliyah Thomas-Pratt

Shanna Yahyahkeekoot

CONTENTS

INTRODUCTION

THE CAUSES OF WORLD WAR ONE

World War One was called the Great War because of how many countries were involved and because 17 million people were killed in the conflict that began on July 28, 1914, and ended on November 11, 1918. The causes are so complicated that historians are unable to come to full agreement, but they do agree that the trigger for the war was the assassination of the archduke of Austria in June of 1914. He was killed by a Serbian student who was part of a revolutionary group that wanted to end Austria–Hungary rule and create a new state of greater Serbia.

Roughly a month later, Austria and Hungary declared war on Serbia. Austria was backed by Germany, and Serbia was backed by Russia. As a result, Germany declared war on Russia.

Russia was part of a defense alliance called the Triple Entente: France, Russia and the United Kingdom of Great Britain and Ireland had all agreed that if one of the countries was attacked, the others would join the fight and would be commonly known as the Allied forces. By declaring war on Russia, Germany was involving these other countries in the war.

In early August, German troops marched on France, taking a route through Belgium, which was a neutral country.

The United Kingdom also had an agreement to defend Belgium, so at this point Britain declared war on Germany. And since Canada in 1914 was part of the British Empire, Canada was now at war with Germany too.

Once the German march on France was stopped, the battle on the Western Front of France and Belgium—the Eastern Front was along the border of the Russian Empire—became a stalemate, largely as a result of something new to warfare: the machine gun.

Traditionally, a mass of soldiers could advance on another mass of soldiers, and eventually one side would overcome the other. A machine gun in the hands of a few soldiers, however, proved to be an overwhelming advantage no matter how large the group of advancing soldiers.

As a result, neither side could find a way to get past the other. Both sides dug trenches deep enough to shelter soldiers from bullets, and sometimes only wide enough for two soldiers to walk side by side. These trenches were sometimes barely more than the length of a football field away from the enemy, close enough that they could communicate by yelling.

With each side dug in and unable to advance on the other, France became the battleground of the Western Front of the Great War.

Bullets whizzed over Jake York. The scouting mission had gone wrong. With the other nineteen soldiers of his platoon, he was crouched behind a small hill, trapped by enemy machine gun fire from the other side.

Worse, from miles away, monstrous artillery guns now fired explosive shells at their location. Their own Canadian guns! Nobody at headquarters knew the platoon had been ambushed at that location, and it was only a matter of time before a shell hit them.

At the dreaded whistling sound of another approaching shell, Jake tried to hug the ground. The shell exploded a couple hundred yards behind, throwing up huge gobs of mud that splashed on his helmet.

On his left side, Jake felt an elbow hit his ribs. He looked over at Charlie Austin, a new soldier to the platoon, tall and skinny.

"Look at him blubber," Charlie said, pointing at another soldier named Mark Lipton. "No wonder you guys call him Princess."

Mark was close enough to hear Charlie. He was the biggest soldier in the platoon, well over six feet tall and as wide as a barrel. He was barely older than a boy and so shy that he blushed if you gave him a direct look. Tears streamed down his face as he curled his huge body around a small cage, as if that could protect the bird inside from two hundred pounds of explosives.

"Charlie," Jake said, "I barely know you, but already I'm done with you."

Jake knew that Mark had been given his nickname back in Canada, at the training camp on a morning that he'd slept late. A sergeant had dumped a bucket of water on Mark and called him Princess in a bellowing voice that had been heard hundreds of yards away, causing laughter among all the soldiers.

But this was not training camp.

It was war. In France. Jake's platoon, called the Storming Normans, was part of one of the four companies that made up the 36th Battalion. They were on the battle line of trenches with tens of thousands of German soldiers on the other side. No one was laughing anymore.

"He's a crybaby," Charlie repeated. "You should be done with him instead."

"Ignore him," Jake told Mark. "Everyone else around here knows how much we need your pigeon."

"Little Abigail," Mark said. "That's what I call her. Little Abigail."

"Something to eat," Charlie said. "That's what I'd call it. Tasty little pigeon."

Mark blinked away fresh tears.

Jake's young face was gray with lack of sleep and smeared with the inescapable mud. He leaned down to pull at the shoelaces of his boots, but his fingers were greasy with mud and he made little progress.

Jake noticed the soldier on the other side of him was watching with a question on his face. All Jake knew so far was the man's name, Thomas Northstar, and that he was Cree from Saskatchewan. Thomas had not spoken once since taking a spot beside Jake. Rumor was that—except to say "yes, sir" to Lieutenant Norman—Thomas hadn't spoken once since joining the platoon.

"Hey," Jake said to Thomas, "you wearing socks with those moccasins?"

Like many Cree in the Canadian Expeditionary Force, Thomas wore moccasins instead of boots. Moccasins were more comfortable and easier for running. Jake was wishing that he had his own pair.

Thomas nodded.

"My boots are too muddy to untie my laces," Jake explained to Thomas. "Any chance you'd give me those socks for important military reasons?"

Thomas shook his head from side to side. Jake had been joking with his question. No soldier gave up socks.

The dreaded whistling sound came again. Jake ducked his head and held his breath. *Whoomp!* This one landed a few yards closer than the previous one.

"I'd heard so much about this platoon of Storming Normans," Charlie said, pulling his head back up. "But if Lieutenant Norman was that good, we wouldn't be stuck here."

"That's why I need my socks," Jake told Thomas. "If he doesn't shut up, I'm going to stuff them in his mouth to stop the complaining."

Thomas broke the silence he'd held since joining the platoon and said to Charlie, "I have not taken off these socks for two weeks. I suggest you listen to Jake or you will not like the taste when I help him feed them to you."

—•—

There was another reason that Mark Lipton was called Princess by his friends. When it came to animals, he had the gentlest touch. He fought tears at the sight of any animal in pain. Any other man might have been teased for it, but Lipton's pain was so visible that to the other soldiers it seemed to express all of the sorrows they had to keep bottled up in these horrible times.

Because of that gentleness, Mark had been given the job of caring for the pigeons. The cage he protected was strung with shoulder straps and held only one pigeon.

There had been four in the cage a day earlier. One at a time, a couple of hours apart, each of the other three had been released. Each had failed to make it past patrolling falcons and German gunners. Little Abigail was Mark's favorite and the only one that remained.

Others said that a pigeon did not recognize men the way that a dog might, and the huge man never disagreed because he was always too shy to argue with anyone. But Mark knew better. He knew that Little Abigail loved eating seed directly from his hand when he reached into the cage, and he knew that Little Abigail loved it when he stroked her feathers at night to calm her before putting a blanket over the cage.

—•—

Lieutenant Norman crawled toward them through a haze of smoke from the explosions, nodding with a grim tightness of his mouth. He was a man of medium build, but something in the intensity of his dark eyes made him seem a lot larger.

"It's time," Lieutenant Norman told Mark. "Last chance."

Mark understood. He'd already watched three not make it, and his tears were for the danger that this one faced. Little Abigail.

Mark fumbled with the clasps to the small door of the wire cage. Mark reached inside to wrap his fingers around the bird, and Little Abigail did not flinch. He felt the softness of the bird's downy breast feathers and the rapid firing of the bird's heart against her ribs.

Mark pulled Little Abigail out of the cage. They both waited for their orders. Because a good soldier—no matter what size—would do what was needed.

—·—

Little Abigail was a beautiful white bird with slate gray markings on her breast and wings. She was born and bred with an ability to find her way home, no matter where she was released.

Outside the cage, to Little Abigail, the hands that held her were huge. But she did not feel fear, because the gentleness of those giant hands was always a comfort to her, giving her a sense of protection. She did not struggle, then, as the large hands cradled her body, and she did not pull her left leg away from the fingers of the other man who carefully tied the tiny tube to the delicate bone.

She waited, because she knew that soon she would be flung into the freedom of flight.

A pigeon cannot understand human words, but it does understand sound and emotion.

"Fly fast and brave," said the man that others called Princess. He brushed his face against the top of her head and opened his hands.

Little Abigail tucked her legs into her belly and burst upward with a flash of wings.

Ahead were falcons that could dive at more than a hundred miles an hour faster than Little Abigail's fastest speed.

But the real danger was in her first moments of flight.

Little Abigail needed to gain height and circle a few times to find her way. When she was oriented, she adjusted her wing tips to make a diving turn and, by nothing more than sheer good fortune, ducked beneath the first bullet fired at her. The shot was so close that a slight puff of feathers blew away in the air currents.

Unfortunately, the next bullet hit more than outer feathers, and Little Abigail tumbled from the sky.

Jake saw her disappear in a small clump of land between the enemy soldiers and the trapped platoon.

—·—

That's it then, Lieutenant John Norman thought. *We are finished.*

Without realizing he had done it, the lieutenant reached inside his uniform and felt the edges of the photograph of his young son. He didn't need to pull it out to see his son's face. Lieutenant Norman had every feature memorized. With his fingers on the photograph, he allowed himself to imagine that he was stepping off a train back home, and that his son was running toward him, arms outstretched.

Lieutenant Norman told himself he would keep this image in his mind for as long as possible. He would fight to the end, but without a message reaching the commanding officers, he would not be stepping off a train in Canada to hold his son.

"Sir," Mark said. "Look."

Mark had not stopped watching the small clump of land where his favorite pigeon had fallen. He'd believed in Little Abigail and refused to give up on her.

Somehow Little Abigail had managed to fight gravity and

pull herself into the gray air. Like an erratic butterfly, she fluttered a few feet from the ground, then ten feet.

It tore at Princess to see the awkwardness of Little Abigail's movements. She was no longer sleek and fast; she was clumsy and heavy. But she had managed to fall out of range of German bullets and was safe from more gunfire.

She climbed. And climbed. Little Abigail was determined to conquer the gravity that wanted to pull her down.

Then, regaining strength and resolution, Little Abigail found her direction and pushed hard toward her home.

—·—

"Sir! Sir!"

An hour later and dozens of miles away, a woman in a Canadian nurse's uniform called for the nearest officer. The bell had just clanged, alerting her to the arrival of a pigeon in the roost.

Her name was Elizabeth Reed, and she had come from Toronto to join the war effort. She was tall with reddish hair, and she loved reading at nights, even though too often it was by candlelight because the electricity was out.

She served at a nearby hospital, but she was visiting the pigeon loft because she volunteered in her spare time to feed the birds and clean the cages. She had been standing near the cage where Little Abigail had been born five months earlier, when, with no warning, Little Abigail had come crashing into the loft with a feeble flapping of wings.

Elizabeth had watched in disbelief as Little Abigail tried to find a perch, then toppled onto the wires of the cage floor. The bird was no longer beautiful white, but red with blood from a torn breast, exhausted to the point of death.

Little Abigail's will to return home was all that had kept her alive, and now that she'd arrived, she was on the verge of succumbing to her wounds.

Unconscious, she was barely alive.

Elizabeth lifted Little Abigail as softly as possible. Her first duty was the message in the tube. Little Abigail had given every ounce of her effort to deliver the message and those efforts would not be wasted.

Elizabeth scanned the message. "It's the location of a platoon from the 36th Battalion. Trapped in the German sector. Under enemy fire and facing our own shells. They need help!"

The officer nodded, then examined the bird. One bullet had torn the bird's breast, another bullet had grazed her eye socket, and a third had smashed and broken a leg.

It was incredible that Little Abigail had managed to fly the distance.

"A shame," the officer said. "It looks like she won't make it."

He tapped the message and spoke again. "But thanks to her, the soldiers might."

—·—

Three weeks later, at the end of her shift at the hospital, Elizabeth Reed walked out to face a sunny afternoon that was warm even for early August. A large man in a Canadian uniform approached her.

He was fumbling with his cap in his hands, twisting it with obvious nervousness, so she gave him a smile for encouragement. This was a soldier on leave. The men would spend two weeks in the trenches, and then be given a full week away from the fighting.

Elizabeth knew how important leave was for the soldiers.

They could shower and get warm, eat a full meal and sleep without worrying about rats crawling into their blankets or shells dropping from the dark sky.

Her smile wasn't enough to set him at ease. He kept looking at his shoes as he twisted his hat.

"Hello," Elizabeth said. "I haven't seen you before. Are you looking for a friend in the hospital?"

For such a huge man, he was extremely quiet.

"Yes," he said, still staring at the ground. "Only . . ."

"Only?"

"It's one of the birds, you see." He finally lifted his eyes to hers. "And I've been told you're the one who made sure she's alive."

That's when Elizabeth understood.

"Little Abigail!" Elizabeth said.

The huge man grinned. "Yes!"

He seemed to lose his shyness as he spoke. "You might not understand. We all thought we were goners. Then, like magic, the shells stopped getting closer. And when . . ."

He stopped. Not from shyness, this time, but from the gratitude that was overwhelming him.

"Yes?" she said.

"And when we saw another Canadian platoon, it was like a miracle. They'd fought their way past the enemy to rescue us. That's when I knew that, somehow, Little Abigail had made it here. So I asked. They said it was you who made a surgeon put her on the operating table."

Elizabeth smiled. "Indeed. Would you like to see her?"

"Yes!" The huge man seemed transformed into a little boy.

"My name is Elizabeth," she said.

"I'm Mark," he answered.

"Come with me," she said.

As he followed her, Elizabeth kept speaking.

"By the way," Elizabeth said. "Have you heard the other news about Little Abigail?"

"No." Suddenly he was nervous again.

"Don't worry," she said. They had reached the bird coop, and sounds of cooing pigeons filled the air. "Look for yourself."

She pointed at a medal hanging from the cage. "It's wonderful news. Everyone knows how plucky she was and how many lives she saved. She's a real war hero. When the French president heard about her, he decided she deserved one of France's great honors—the Croix de Guerre."

The Cross of War! Mark felt like his face was splitting from the huge grin that hit him. But he was more concerned about seeing Abigail than admiring the medal.

There she was in the corner, head tilted and a gleam in her eyes.

"I'd like to hold her," Mark said. "Would that be all right?"

"Of course," Elizabeth said.

Mark reached into the cage. Abigail allowed his big hands to fold around her. He pulled her out. That's when he noticed that someone had carved her a wooden leg to replace the one that had been shattered by a bullet.

He didn't even care that his eyes filled with tears and he was crying in front of a woman he'd just met.

CHER AMI

THE INSPIRATION
BEHIND THE STORY OF
LITTLE ABIGAIL

On October 4, 1918, US Army Major Charles Whittlesey and two hundred soldiers were trapped in a small depression on a hillside. This was their second day of battle, and they were in a desperate situation. Incoming fire from their own artillery, meant to help protect them, was instead landing closer and closer because their precise position was unknown.

Major Whittlesey had sent out a number of pigeons over the span of the battle, and his final bird was named Cher Ami, which means "dear friend" in French. Cher Ami had been on the front line for several months and had already flown twelve missions.

When Cher Ami was released, enemy gunners were waiting and fired such a volley that three bullets struck the bird. One bullet blinded Cher Ami. A second bullet tore through his chest. And a third bullet shattered his leg.

Cher Ami fluttered to the ground. Then, to the soldiers' disbelief and joy, Cher Ami struggled back into the air and flew

forty kilometers (25 mi.) to deliver the message, saving the trapped soldiers.

Medics from the 77th Infantry Division saved Cher Ami's life but could not save his shattered leg, so they carved him a wooden leg as a replacement. French soldiers heard of the brave bird and awarded Cher Ami one of the highest medals of honor in the French army.

Later, Cher Ami was sent to the United States and received a hero's welcome. When Cher Ami died about a year later, his body was preserved and put on display at the Smithsonian American History Museum in Washington, D.C.

THE CARRIER PIGEON IN WAR

With the ability to deliver messages at speeds of up to one hundred kilometers (62 mi.) an hour, carrier pigeons were a vital part of World War One communications. Once released, the pigeons had to avoid enemy fire and the enemy's trained falcons. Over 100,000 pigeons were used during the war, and they had an astounding success rate of 95 percent.

The pigeons were kept in mobile lofts behind the front line, drawn either by horses or automobiles, then taken into the trenches as necessary. Pigeons delivered messages from ship to ship as well, and were even sent from airplanes. They were also released with messages when sailors or pilots faced shipwrecks or crashes. One pigeon, launched from a ship wrecked out at sea, managed to deliver a message 305 kilometers (190 mi.).

The importance of the pigeons in the war was such that nearly thirty years later, despite many advances in technology, there were double the number of pigeon messengers in World War Two.

COMMUNICATION DIFFICULTIES IN WORLD WAR ONE

Communications were crucial to coordinating the efforts of tens of thousands of soldiers. Messages had to be sent and received to warn of ambushes and enemy presence, to shift soldiers to new locations during battle and to ensure that soldiers knew what orders to follow.

Traditionally, armies communicated with flag signals and messengers on foot or horseback, but telephone and telegraph had been introduced. These were not new technologies. Telephone was preferred, as it offered immediate two-way communication. But this kind of communication meant having to lay hundreds of kilometers of wire throughout the trenches, usually buried a minimum of thirty centimeters (12 in.). Also, the enemy was capable of listening to conversations; until the introduction of insulated lines, all it took was adding a wire on the ground nearby to intercept messages.

Laying wire also came at a tremendous cost of lives. During major offensive operations, engineers scrambled to lay wire or replace wire destroyed by shelling, putting themselves in the line of fire. For the British Royal Engineers Signal Service, as an example, the casualty rates were sometimes as high as 50 percent.

Worse, when soldiers had advanced or retreated, they moved away from the wires, basically cutting off their communication.

As the war went on, the armies on both sides began to try wireless units. Although wireless, they weren't exactly portable. In 1916, a wireless

set for an aircraft weighed over 136 kilograms (300 lb.) and required an antenna dangling from the airplane that was 137 meters (450 ft.) long.

In the trenches, an operator carrying a wireless set needed the assistance of two helpers, each carrying antenna wires. One would walk fifteen meters (50 ft.) in front and the other the same distance behind.

It is no wonder then that so many lives depended on animal messengers, including dogs and carrier pigeons, for reliable and fast delivery of messages.

UNDERSTANDING HOW CARRIER PIGEONS DELIVER MESSAGES

Sending a message via carrier pigeon, often called "Pigeon Post," usually consists of writing a message on thin, light paper that is then rolled into a small tube and attached to the bird's leg.

However, some pigeons are trained to carry up to seventy-five grams (2.5 oz.) on their backs. In England and France as recently as the 1980s, pigeons were used to transport medical samples between hospitals for the simple reason that it was much faster and more efficient for a bird to fly direct than sending human couriers in cars or on bikes on crowded roads.

Once in the air, the pigeon orients itself and travels the shortest route possible to its home base. Some researchers believe the birds rely on the Earth's magnetic field to form a mental map and compass. The researchers have learned that the top of the pigeon's beak has a large amount of iron particles, and they believe that these particles align themselves to face the north, no differently than compasses used by humans.

Other researchers, however, think that pigeons use sound frequencies below what humans can sense to understand location. They believe that the length of sound waves at this level  explains why a pigeon must circle a few times before leaving: the pigeon has to mentally map the sound. Researchers have also been able to use these sound waves to disrupt or even redirect a pigeon's navigation.

Regardless of how pigeons are able to find their way home, there is no doubt that those who merely see them as urban pests are missing what makes them so fascinating.

During any other time in his life and at any other place, it would have been impossible for Jake to sleep in the conditions of the trench. He'd grown up on a farm in Manitoba, sharing a bedroom with two little brothers. His bed was warm and dry, and the only sounds at night would be coyotes outside and the gentle snoring of his little brothers sharing the other bed in the room.

For all of his teenage years, he'd thought the farm was boring. He fell asleep each night dreaming of adventure that would come when he could finally leave it. Until his first few nights in a trench, he'd had no idea how wonderful the peace and security of his own bedroom had been.

His first nights in the trench seemed like years ago to Jake instead of just months. Then, sleep had been impossible. The muck was a thick goo that sometimes pulled his boots loose. When it rained, all he had for protection was his helmet and overcoat. Attack from the enemy coming over the top of the trench could happen at any moment. Sometimes artillery fire was so intense that a soldier could read a newspaper by the light from the constant explosions.

But very soon, Jake, like all the soldiers, had discovered that exhaustion could overcome all of that and that they could sleep through almost anything, even dread.

Tonight, in a few hours, Jake would be sent on a mission to No Man's Land—the area between their trenches and the trenches of the enemy. Jake should have been too nervous to sleep. But his body needed sleep so badly that he didn't care about the danger ahead.

Even though other soldiers tramped past him, he was asleep within seconds of lying on a board across the top of the mud. He began to dream about Thanksgiving dinner, where he was smiling at his little brothers as he helped carve a roast turkey. In his dream, he began to explain to everyone at the table that he'd never understood how something as simple as a dinner with family could be one of the most enjoyable things in life.

But the dream lost its joy when a hideously large rat popped out of the inside of the roast turkey and crawled up his arm. His family ignored the rat and pleasantly continued their conversations. Jake's throat was frozen by shock and it seemed he couldn't move his arm, and the rat kept climbing. Onto his shoulder. Onto his face.

The dream was so real that Jake felt the clammy cold feet of that rat on the skin of his cheek, then felt a tickle of whiskers across his forehead. He was just starting to realize that it was more than a dream when a sharp pain tore through the lobe of his left ear.

A rat had just bitten him!

He thrashed his arms to slap at his face, and the rat disappeared in a flash.

Yes, in the trenches, a soldier could sleep through almost anything. Except for the visits from rats.

At night, they scurried everywhere: from within the bags of grain for horses to under blankets and inside backpacks. More and more, though, the Storming Normans were facing fewer rats. This was the first one to bite Jake in a week, thanks to a cat named Boomer who patrolled the trenches.

Jake rubbed his ear and tried to fall asleep again, but his heart was pounding. His exhaustion was overwhelming, and he needed sleep to be alert for his mission tonight.

With his eyes open in the dark, waiting for the dreaded appearance of another rat, it seemed like he was hearing an unfamiliar noise. It took him a few moments to realize it was the sound of a man quietly sobbing.

To one side of Jake, Thomas Northstar snored gently. It seemed Thomas could sleep through anything. Nothing frightened or disturbed him. Except spiders. And that was a different story altogether.

The sobbing came from Jake's other side.

Charlie Austin. Blundering, blustering Charlie Austin. Tonight would be Charlie's first mission out into No Man's Land.

Jake's reaction was not scorn, but sympathy. He wondered if he should try to talk to Charlie. Maybe not now. Later. Now was the time to try to sleep. Jake needed the sleep to be alert in a few hours when he went into No Man's Land. His life depended on it. And the lives of other soldiers in the platoon depended on him.

Jake closed his eyes and forced himself to breathe with long, slow breaths. Then he heard a sharp, short squeal.

That put a smile on Jake's face.

Boomer had just added one more to the count. Jake hoped it was the rat that had just nipped at his ear.

Jake began to relax again and drifted into sleep.

———•———

Farther down the trench, Justin Biggs also woke to a soft touch of whiskers across the forehead. These whiskers made him smile; he knew they belonged to his cat, Boomer.

Justin had been out in No Man's Land on the previous night's mission. It would be a while until it was his turn again, so he wasn't quite as desperate for sleep as Jake. Besides, Justin never minded when Boomer returned to him.

He also knew why Boomer was back.

Boomer was a black and white cat with a scar over his right eye. Justin had rescued the cat from a huge dog back in one of the French towns when he was on leave. His cat loved him as much he loved his cat. No doubt Boomer had just brought him a present: a dead rat. This gift from Boomer showed that the cat wanted to help out by sharing his food with his friend.

The war had turned life upside down from Justin's previous world as a math teacher in an elementary school in Berlin, Ontario. It was so upside down that some of the letters from home told him that many people in the city wanted to change the city's name because it had the same name as the city in Germany.

Back in Canada, before the war, Justin would have been horrified at the sight of a rat, and even more horrified to have one dropped beside him as he was sleeping.

Not here.

Boomer had already returned ten times tonight and would soon prowl for more. In the morning, the soldiers would count them all and cheer for Boomer. One of the lucky soldiers would win the jackpot, because every night Justin ran a pool for those who wanted to pay a few pennies to guess how many hated rats Boomer would remove from the trenches.

Boomer pushed his face hard against Justin's face and rubbed. Someone had once told Justin it was so that Boomer could mark Justin's face with scent from glands on the cat's face. It meant that Boomer regarded Justin as his property.

If it was true, Justin was just fine with that. It didn't matter to him if he belonged to Boomer, or Boomer belonged to him. As long as they were together.

Boomer purred for a few moments against the side of Justin's face, then slipped into the night to hunt.

—·—

Too soon, Jake's sleep ended.

Lieutenant Norman was above him, tapping his shoulder.

Jake sat up and yawned.

Lieutenant Norman moved to Charlie Austin and tapped Charlie too.

"You have your orders, York," Lieutenant Norman said to Jake. The officer was just a dark outline. His voice was soft. "Repeat them back to me."

"Three hours of observation at the post at the halfway mark," Jake said.

"And?" Lieutenant Norman said.

"Sir?" Jake said. He didn't know anything else had been added to the orders.

"Return safely," Lieutenant Norman said. "This platoon needs both of you."

The returning safely, Jake knew, was an unnecessary order. Everyone did their best to return safely. It was Lieutenant Norman's way of telling his soldiers that he cared about them.

"Yes, sir," Jake said.

"Austin," Lieutenant Norman said. "Cat got your tongue? If so, I wouldn't be surprised if Boomer is the guilty one. Notice that the rats are nearly gone from our part of the trenches?"

"Sir," Charlie began in a weak voice, "it's just that I don't want to . . ."

Jake had a horrible feeling that Charlie was going to try to beg not to go. That would lead to a shame that Charlie would never forget.

Jake jumped back into the conversation.

"Lieutenant Norman," Jake said, "I'm with Charlie. I don't want to see any more rats for as long as I live. So while we're out there, we'll be cheering for Boomer to get rid of as many rats as possible."

"Cheer silently," Lieutenant Norman said. "I want you back."

"Of course, sir," Jake said. He kept talking so that Charlie couldn't interrupt. "I've got my bet placed on the number twenty-three for the night. What's your number, sir?"

"Seventeen. Boomer is amazing, but no cat is good enough to make it past twenty. Some of those rats are almost as big as a cat. Too bad we can't shoot at them in the trenches."

"Yes, sir," Jake said.

Jake nudged Charlie. Jake didn't like Charlie much, but in Lieutenant Norman's platoon, all the soldiers worked together. Also, Jake could feel sympathy for any man's fears in this horrible war.

"I've done this a dozen times," Jake told Charlie. "I'll make sure you're okay out there."

The two of them slipped over the top of the trench and into the night to hunt.

—•—

The rat was nearly three years old and weighed as much as a small cat. The darkness around the rat was like a blanket of comfort. Vision didn't mean much to the rat. In daylight, beyond a few feet everything was blurry anyway, and the rat only looked for large moving objects.

That's why it inflicted its reign over the soldiers at night. It crawled along the side of the trench, using its whiskers to brush the sandbags. It navigated by touch.

Its whiskers bent against a brass casing from a rifle shot. Two whiskers flicked the casing. The direction of the bend of the hair and how much each hair bent was enough for the rat to visualize the object as if it were in bright sunlight.

The rat froze briefly, lifting its head to try to detect danger. Incredibly, it could also detect sound through its whiskers. Shorter whiskers near its nose vibrated with higher-pitched sounds than the longer whiskers farther back. Its brain could read those vibrations like its ears understood sound.

Safe.

Its nose held another and larger scent gland, primarily for the scent of animals, especially other rats. Every few steps, the rat secreted tiny drops of urine to mark its trail, and every few steps it inhaled the smell of the urine of rats that had passed by earlier, knowing the age and identity of those rats, even how stressed each had been.

He smelled fear in the other rat's urine. Fear of a predator. What kind of predator? Not human. A rat could easily dodge a human.

It froze again, listening carefully with ears and whiskers for the slightest indication of that predator. This rat had made it to the age of three because it was cunning and careful.

It moved forward again. It was not driven by hunger, but by a lust for blood. Human blood.

Rats developed a taste for fresh human blood, and the only way to get it was to nibble, bite and suck as the soldiers slept.

Occasionally, its prey managed to slap the rat away with great violence.

But that didn't matter. A rat heard a sound as slight as a human rubbing a thumb against a finger, so it was almost impossible to surprise.

This rat, like all the other rats in the trenches, was superb at survival, no matter how hard humans tried to exterminate it. And it was superb at inflicting misery on those humans in revenge for their efforts. It was able to slip into the tiniest of holes, and, with its tail for balance, was able to climb nearly anything. No wonder legions of rats could swarm the trenches unharmed.

Yes. This rat wanted blood. With another wiggle of whiskers, it slipped forward in the night to hunt.

—•—

Crawling among the craters of the battle-scarred mud of No Man's Land, Jake and Charlie had joined the horrible game that many of the soldiers called "blindfold cat and mouse."

Not Jake.

He always called it "blindfold cat and rat," knowing he had one enemy in his own trenches that tried to eat him while he slept, and another in the trenches on the other side of No Man's Land that tried to shoot him as he moved.

By this time in the war, the trenches had reached a stalemate. In some places, the opposing lines were barely more than a football field apart. Neither army could move forward and neither would retreat.

But far beneath the mud, thousands of each side's sappers—these were mine diggers who were also called moles or sewer rats—sent a spiderweb of tunnels toward the opposing side. The goal was to dig beneath the enemy trench and fill the hole with explosives.

The only defense was to lie on the ground above and listen for the sound of pickaxes below, then report back to command on the location of an enemy's approaching tunnel.

Jake and Charlie each wore wristwatches with glowing faces. Twenty minutes was the rotation. With volleys of bullets going overhead, Jake would press his ear to the ground and hold it there, straining to hear any vibrations. It was Charlie's job to remain crouched and watch for enemy patrols, for at night, safe from snipers, was when patrols moved through No Man's Land.

After five minutes, Jake shook from the wet, cold mud. He had no choice but to remain on his belly until Charlie tapped his shoulder at the end of the twenty-minute shift.

Charlie slid onto his belly. Jack knelt in a crouch to watch for patrols. Then no more bullets overhead. Silence.

"Finally," Charlie whispered. "They've stopped shoot—"

He didn't get out another sound. Jake had slammed a hand against Charlie's mouth.

Jake leaned in close, putting his lips against Charlie's ear and murmuring in a tone that could barely be heard.

"When they stop shooting," Jake said, "it's because they've sent out their own patrol."

Then Jake heard it. Boots in the mud. At least twenty soldiers. They loomed out of the darkness, barely yards away.

—•—

Unlike a dog, a cat is a cautious creature, measuring its odds in any fight. Dogs charge headlong at a larger opponent, drawing admiration for heart. Cats avoid fights they will lose, drawing admiration for intelligence.

Boomer, however, had a remarkable combination of heart and intelligence. Boomer loved to attack rats, despite their large size and ferocious fighting abilities.

Boomer was a warrior. Skill for skill, he matched the large rat that had so recently scurried along the trench wall to seek soldiers' blood.

As Boomer hunted, each of his paws came down so silently and so softly that it was impossible for a rat's keen hearing to detect his approach, either by sound or vibration. Boomer never straightened his legs completely but moved in a graceful prowl, even at full speed. His body was a machine capable of leaping five times his body height from a standstill.

With each crouching step forward, Boomer swiveled his outer ear flaps. Like an incredible piece of engineering, the thirty-two ear muscles allowed Boomer to twist his ears in a half circle, similar to a radar dish scanning for vibrations. Boomer's inner ear had a special organ to control balance, so finely tuned that he could instantly spin and land on his feet from even the shortest of drops.

Yet Boomer did not depend on hearing to locate the rat. At least not from a distance.

He used his nose, which contained 200 million nerve cells, compared to a human's 5 million. As Boomer took each stealthy step, he curled back his upper lip, drawing in smells that mapped out the trench in the dark. To him, the fresh tiny drops of rat urine were like flashing lights on a dark runway, guiding him closer and closer to the skulking rat.

Each slight air current told Boomer something new. His whiskers could match a rat's whiskers for sensitivity, twelve whiskers like probing antennae on each side of his face.

As Boomer followed the trail left behind by the rat, he moved into the current, knowing that the air would take his scent behind him and not alert the rat in front of him.

Closer and closer Boomer moved, but so silently the rat had no idea of approaching danger.

Boomer's greatest advantage over the rat was vision. Boomer could open the pupils of his eyes three times more than a human, and as a result only needed one-sixth of the light that a human did to be able to see with the same clarity.

That's how—when he was within pouncing distance of his prey—Boomer saw the rat where it was perched at the feet of a sleeping solider, ready to crawl up the man's pant leg.

The rat was huge.

Yet Boomer, true soldier that he was, prepared for battle and dropped into a crouch of attack anyway.

—•—

Jake remained frozen in a half crouch. He held his rifle at waist height, focused on the movement of the patrol. He was grateful for the mud that caked his uniform; it made him invisible.

Lifting one hand from his rifle, Jake made a motion for Charlie to stay down on his belly.

Jake would fight if needed, but the odds were against them. Gunfire would alert the enemy back in the trenches to their location, and the mission would be a failure.

He moved his hand back to his rifle. Jake didn't dare click off the safety. The soldiers of the patrol were too close. They would hear it.

Jake felt the rush of blood in his veins, thinking that it must be as loud to the enemy as it was to him. He expected one of them to turn and point and shout a command to shoot.

One of the soldiers stopped and did a half turn, as if he could sense Jake nearby in the dark. Jake stopped breathing. He willed himself to remain a statue.

Seconds ticked by. Finally the enemy soldier moved away, and all of them began to disappear into the darkness.

For now, the danger had ended.

Just as Jake relaxed, he heard a splash. Then the low rumble of cursing.

Jake froze, then swallowed a laugh as he realized what had happened. Some of the enemy soldiers had fallen into the water at the bottom of a shell crater. Maybe later, if he lived long enough, he'd tell Thomas and the rest of the platoon. But only after they completed their mission.

Jake knelt and murmured again into Charlie's ear.

"They're gone. Keep listening for sappers," Jake whispered. "The platoon is depending on us."

—•—

The rat moved forward, excited by the overwhelming smells that came from the body of its living human prey. It had lived long and well because of its skills and stealth, and now it wanted another reward for venturing down the trench.

Behind the rat, however, Boomer was crouched, with a twitching tail. Boomer let his muscles ripple beneath his fur, warming those muscles to unleash power like a racehorse out of the gate.

The rat took one step onto the sleeping soldier's leg. Its final step.

Boomer launched with the precision of an arrow and drove into the rat's body.

It didn't even have time to squeal.

———•———

At dawn, back in the trench, Jake and Charlie stretched their cold muscles as the rest of the platoon woke to the call of "Stand To."

"Good work out there," Lieutenant Norman told Jake and Charlie. "After inspection, find a place to sleep. You deserve it."

"I need a hot bath," Charlie said.

"That's what I like in a soldier," Lieutenant Norman said. "A sense of humor."

Lieutenant Norman walked away.

"I wasn't joking," Charlie told Jake. "I hate this."

"Then doing it makes you a good soldier," Jake said, thinking of how Charlie had been crying in the dark. "It's too easy to do things you like. And brave to do something when you're afraid."

By the look on Charlie's face, Jake realized he had just made himself an enemy.

"I'm never afraid," Charlie said, scowling. "And I'll fight you if you go around telling that to others."

Before Jake could say anything, Lieutenant Norman turned back to them and interrupted the conversation.

"Oh, by the way," Lieutenant Norman said to Jake. "You might want to save some of your breakfast as a reward for Boomer. You just won the bet. Twenty-three rats last night. Word has it that's a record for any platoon."

"Thank you, sir," Jake said.

Jake wanted to talk to Charlie more about bravery, but Charlie followed Lieutenant Norman down the trench.

That was too bad. Jake wanted Charlie to know that he was always afraid out there too.

PITOUCHI AND SIMON

THE INSPIRATION BEHIND THE STORY OF
BOOMER

A soldier in the Belgian army named Lieutenant Lekeux adopted an orphan kitten and named it Pitouchi. As the kitten grew, it followed Lekeux everywhere.

Months later, Lekeux was near the German lines and saw the enemy soldiers digging a new trench. He hid nearby and began to make drawings. He was so intent on his work that he didn't see German soldiers approach until it was too late.

He tried to hide by lying as still as possible, but they had spotted his movement. As they were about to shoot, Pitouchi jumped out and startled the soldiers, who shot at the cat and missed. The soldiers joked that they had mistaken a cat for a man and walked away, leaving Lieutenant Lekeux safe.

Boomer's amazing hunting abilities and determination are based on the 500,000 cats the British Army had in the trenches to keep the rats at bay. One particularly heroic cat named Simon performed the same duty on a ship. He survived a bombing attack that shredded his face, back and left side with shrapnel and burned his eyebrows and whiskers away. While he was recovering, rats infested the ship, invading food supplies and living quarters. As soon as Simon recovered, however, it took him only a matter of days to clear the ship, all except for one monster rat. This rat was smart enough to avoid all the traps the soldiers set, but in the end, Simon overcame this formidable foe.

Simon received three medals for bravery: the Animal Victoria Cross, the Dickin Medal and the Blue Cross Medal.

SAPPERS

During the Great War, tunnel warfare was a large and mostly unseen part of battle. It began on December 21, 1914, when German forces dug a tunnel beneath No Man's Land—the landscape between opposing trenches that had been blasted clear

of trees and bush—to a spot beneath the British trenches and left behind ten bombs, causing tremendous damage.

The British soon formed tunneling units, and by the middle of 1916, the British Army had 25,000 men, many of them from coal-mining communities, trained in digging a network of tunnels. It required nearly 50,000 soldiers to support the men in the tunnels.

Conditions were extremely dangerous. The tunnels were small and often flooded with water. Tunnels could collapse at any time. Sappers from one side would sometimes break into a tunnel of sappers from the other side, resulting in savage underground battles. Some gases emitted from the soil were explosive—dangerous because sappers worked by candle-light. Carbon monoxide gas was a silent killer. Animals were innocent heroes in tunnels too: sappers brought down mice and small birds, such as canaries, to help detect the gases.

On the surface, soldiers would listen for enemy sappers in a variety of ways. Some would drive a stick in the ground and hold it in their teeth to feel for vibrations. Others used medical stethoscopes.

The stakes were high. At Vimy Ridge, the Germans had an extensive network of mines and deep tunnels in place to attack French positions, and it was important to neutralize this threat before the final battle in April 1917.

RATS

Rats can survive drops of fifteen meters (50 ft.), tread water for three days and live through being flushed down a toilet. Rats are also difficult to poison, as they are intelligent enough to try new foods in small doses. One pair of rats can produce up to two thousand descendants in a single year; there were an estimated 10 million rats in the trenches during World War One.

And these rats found plenty to eat. Soldiers heaved their empty food cans over the tops of the trenches—thousands per day. Rats were so bold they would steal food that had been set down for just a second. Given their toughness and ability to reproduce, rats thrived in the trenches, sometimes growing to the size of a cat.

Rats do like human blood. A 1945 study concluded that rats can develop a real craving for fresh human blood. Another study showed that rats most often attack humans between midnight and eight a.m., chewing on faces or hands to seek that blood.

With soldiers so exhausted in the trenches, rats made the problem worse by either waking soldiers up constantly or taking advantage of those too tired to wake up.

Soldiers were not allowed to shoot at rats because it was a waste of ammunition. So, without the cats and ratting dogs to help protect the soldiers, trench conditions would have been far, far worse.

LIFE IN THE TRENCHES

The long, narrow trenches were dug into the ground and lined with sandbags to keep the walls from falling in, and more sandbags were added along the top to add height.

The dangerous and busy hours were at night, when soldiers dug new trenches under the cover of darkness or climbed out of the trenches to repair barbed wire in No Man's Land. Night was also the time to listen for enemy miners. Later in the war, Canadian troops became experts at nighttime raids of the enemy's trenches.

During the day, much of a soldier's life in the trench was a routine of work and rest. Dawn was the usual time for an enemy attack, so the first matter of the day was "Stand To," when soldiers woke to guard the trenches. If no enemy attack came, soldiers faced inspections and breakfast.

Breakfast was followed by tedious chores like cleaning latrines (outdoor bathrooms) or filling and replacing sandbags.

 Soldiers needed to be constantly on guard for enemy snipers, gas attacks and incoming shells. In a unit of eight hundred soldiers, each month it was expected that eighty of them would not survive, so replacements were constantly arriving and learning trench life.

Aside from constant attack by rats and lice, the weather made life miserable for soldiers; they were always cold and wet. Many soldiers developed trench foot: a condition in which constant dampness made feet numb and led to blisters, open sores and fungal infections. If trench foot went untreated, soldiers' feet would have to be amputated. To prevent it, soldiers would form pairs to inspect and apply whale oil to each other's feet.

COAL DUST

"Hear that?" Jake said to Thomas. "The horses. Reminds me of the farm."

Ten kilometers (6 mi.) behind the lines of trenches that formed the war front, Jake and the platoon rested at a barn that been converted into a place where eighty men could sleep.

Outside the barn, in pleasant sunshine, Thomas sat on an old crate, facing a crate in the center. Jake sat across on another crate. They'd finished breakfast: hard biscuits, cheese and something that the cook tried to tell them was bacon, and each had a cup of tea. From the field behind came the occasional neighing of a horse.

"It reminds me of wheelbarrows," Thomas said. "Many horses. Much poop. I would like it very much to find a way to avoid those wheelbarrows."

"Better here with shovels than at the front with rifles," Jake said.

Thomas nodded agreement, even though the straw mattresses were infested with fleas, the floor was dirt, and cracks in the walls let in rain and wind.

To the Storming Normans platoon, it was like a luxury hotel.

They were on leave from fighting at the front. Every platoon followed a rotation. Six days in the trenches, then twelve days behind the trenches. In the trenches, it was mud and rats and keeping watch through the night, then trying to sleep sitting up or standing during the day while shells constantly exploded around them. Away from the trenches, there was a daily routine of work like feeding animals, digging or helping with transportation of goods.

"I think I will be hearing another sound very soon," Thomas said.

"Yes?" Jake asked.

Thomas pointed at the chessboard on the crate between them. "The sound of you crying when I defeat you once again."

"Watch out for that spider on your shoulder," Jake told Thomas.

"Nice try," Thomas said. "You will not be able to distract me from my mission to take your king."

Jake reached forward and plucked the spider from Thomas's shoulder. Jake let the wriggling spider cross his open palm in front of Thomas.

Thomas shuddered and closed his eyes. "Thank you, my friend. Promise me when I open my eyes that this monster of evil will be gone."

Jake set the spider on the ground and let it walk away. There was too much dying in war. No sense in killing something innocent.

"Gone," Jake said. "You're safe, you big baby. Remind me again about the bishop."

Thomas opened his eyes and looked at the board. He leaned over and touched the top of a bishop. "It moves forward or backward on its own color. Diagonally. See how it can reach this pawn?"

Thomas lifted the bishop, moved it down the board to tap the pawn, then replaced the bishop to its original position. "But do not make that move. It would leave your queen in a weak position because of my knight."

"The one that moves two squares one direction and another square in a different direction?" Jake asked.

"That is right. The queen can make all moves of all pieces except the knight."

Jake studied the board, then lifted his head to look at Thomas. "You know, I signed up to fight, not take care of animals. I grew up on a farm and I wanted to get away from animals. Don't get me wrong. Fighting isn't as great as I thought it would be, and I'm happy to be out of the trenches for a few days. But of all the duties to pull, I'm back with horses."

Jake stopped talking to move a pawn, then said, "Worse, we're stuck with Charlie. He tries to do as little work as possible."

"Now your king is in mortal danger," Thomas said. "You may replace the piece and try another move."

Jake moved the pawn back and spoke as he looked at the chess pieces. "Why did you sign up?"

Thomas didn't answer.

"Go ahead and use oxygen to speak," Jake said. "The sky has lots of it."

"Except for when it has been replaced with poison gas."

"Just when we were having fun," Jake said, "you bring that up."

Jake moved a castle.

Thomas sighed and moved his queen. "Remember that word I taught you?"

"Checkmate?" Jake said.

"Yes. That word."

"Again? So soon?"

"Yes," Thomas said. He pointed. "Checkmate."

"I like this game," Jake said. "Give me another chance."

Jake began setting up the board.

Thomas said, "I first saw this game at my residential school. The priests seemed like stealthy hunters when they played, staring at the board like a soaring hawk peering down for mice. I wondered what it was, but they refused to explain. They said a Cree boy was not smart enough for such a game. Naturally, that made me angry. So I found ways to watch them play when they did not know I was nearby. I was smart enough for that. I learned how each piece moves by studying the priests as they played."

Thomas's face had been angry as he spoke, but then he smiled. "It was my grandfather William who taught me the strategy of the game. He learned it at many campfires from a North West Mounted Policeman when Saskatchewan was a territory. He saved the policeman's life once, but I will tell you that story another day."

A frown returned to Thomas's face. "I do not like my memories of the residential school. The Cree and Soto from my home do not deserve the treatment we receive there. When Kaneonuskatew signed the treaty—"

"Did you just sneeze?" Jake asked. "Kanawhatsky?"

"Do not hurt your tongue by twisting it. You are only a farm boy from Manitoba, so I will not take your ignorance as an insult. Besides that, you just saved my life from a spider capable of taking out an entire platoon. Kaneonuskatew means One Who Walks on Four Claws. In English he is known as George Gordon. And he was the first to sign the treaty with Queen Victoria. We expect that we should be treated as equals and thus we are also fighting for Canada as equals. I dream that when we get home we will finally be treated as you are. As citizens."

Jake scratched his head to think about it. He hoped it was just an itch and not a flea. Before he could respond, Charlie Austin reached them with a wheelbarrow.

"Horse poop," Charlie said.

"No," Jake said. "I think that Thomas is right to be angry. The Cree and Soto deserve to be citizens of our country."

"Huh?" Charlie said. "I'm here because it's your turn to shovel horse poop."

"Good thing you left some behind," Jake said. Jake noticed the wheelbarrow was only half full of horse manure. "Otherwise what work would I have?"

Charlie looked at the chessboard and said to Jake, "Why are you wasting time trying to teach Thomas something complicated like chess? Indians are just good for scouting or as snipers."

"You assume I am good at those things just because I am of the Kaneonuskatew Nation?" Thomas asked.

"If that means Indian or redskin, I'd say yes."

"Any man—white or red—who spends a boyhood in the forests and fields with guns to track animals will be good for scouting or shooting," Thomas said. "You grew up in the city. I grew up in the woods. That will give me an advantage over you in scouting or with rifles. It has little to do with color of skin."

"Wrong," Charlie said. "Indians know Indian stuff. It's in the blood. Like with chess for me. I have a natural advantage over you. Because chess needs thinking, not tracking."

"I've been teaching Thomas plenty about chess," Jake said. "He might surprise you with how good he is."

Jake scratched his head again. He grimaced. It *was* a flea.

"In fact," Jake said, "he might even be able to beat you."

"Not a chance," Charlie said. "An Indian?"

"How about this?" Jake said. "You play him right now, and if you win, I'll shovel horse poop for you all week. If you lose, you do all that work for me."

"Are you sure?" Thomas said. "This should be a fair bet."

"Too late," Charlie said. He reached over and moved a pawn. "Jake made the bet and I'm taking it. I'm white. I start first."

"Why is that?" Thomas asked.

"I just explained. I'm white."

Thomas pointed to the black bishop. "Jake, tell me again how this piece moves. What is it called again?"

"A bishop," Jake told Thomas. Jake hid his smile. "Try to remember. It moves on the black squares in a diagonal."

"Explain to me again what is a diagonal," Thomas said.

Charlie rubbed his hands. "This is going to be good. Too bad I didn't bet more."

"I'm willing to take a chance on Thomas," Jake said. "How about we bet your supper for the next two nights as well?"

"Deal," Charlie said.

"I still do not think this is a fair bet," Thomas said.

Thomas was right. The game only lasted fourteen moves. Like they said back home, Thomas beat Charlie like Charlie was leather stretched across a ceremonial drum.

—·—

"Didn't you say you wouldn't be back?"

This came from Lance Wesley, who found an angry Charlie with a shovel, scooping horse manure into a wheelbarrow.

Lance Wesley was a broad-shouldered man with a square face. He carried himself like the former policeman that he was. Lance was holding the reins to his horse, Coal Dust.

"I don't want to talk about it," Charlie said in answer to Lance's question.

"You mean you don't want to talk about how you bragged you were going to leave most of the work for Jake York and Thomas Northstar?" Lance asked.

Beside him, Coal Dust stamped an impatient front foot. The horse got his name because he was coal black. Coal Dust was glossy and rippled with muscles, which was a good indication that he had reached the war only a few weeks earlier. Conditions were so difficult that, after a few months, most horses suffered badly. Another reason for Coal Dust's health was Lance Wesley, who spent hours looking after and grooming him.

"I don't want to talk about it," Charlie said.

"Do you want to talk about how Thomas Northstar beat you at chess in fourteen moves?" Lance asked. "Everyone else is talking about it."

Charlie didn't answer.

Lance said, "Let me give you some advice, okay?"

"No thanks."

Lance said, "What's the name of our platoon?"

"The Storming Normans."

"Notice how much the men respect the lieutenant?" As Lance spoke, Coal Dust nuzzled the big man's shoulder and Lance rubbed the horse's nose.

"I noticed that in my first few days with the platoon we got trapped by the enemy," Charlie answered. "I noticed it took a stupid pigeon to save us."

Lance said, "Then what you didn't notice was that when the attack started, Lieutenant Norman managed to get us to a safe place where we could defend ourselves until the other platoons showed up. Without the lieutenant, we wouldn't have lasted an hour out there. I can tell you it's a good thing he's Canadian and that we're Canadian."

Charlie stopped shoveling and showed his first sign of interest. "Why?"

"Sometimes British officers are chosen because of their family connections. Not Canadians. Canadians get their stripes

49

because they earn it. Sometimes British officers don't make good decisions because they go by the book. They'll send soldiers over the top from a trench in a mad rush because in the old days of war, before machine guns, that's how you did it. Canadian officers like to think for themselves. They find a different way to do something when it looks like the old way won't do it. That's why Canada told the British we'd keep our troops together, not let British officers lead us. We come from prairies and woods and we're tough against cold and as much hard work as you can throw at us. You should feel good about that."

"I'm filling a wheelbarrow with horse poop. I don't feel good about that. I wasn't born for this kind of work. I deserve better."

"There's your problem. Want to fit in? Drop the attitude. If it takes shoveling horse poop to win the war, then it needs to be done without complaint."

"I don't have to listen to you," Charlie said. His resentment was back in his voice.

Lance used his hand to rub the nose of his horse again. Coal Dust lifted his magnificent head and exhaled gently on Lance. Lance let out a deep breath directly into Coal Dust's nostrils.

"What is that?" Charlie said. "Are you two in love?"

Lance smiled. "In a sense, maybe. Horses have amazing smell. We bond through that, smelling each other. Actually, Coal Dust bonds when I let him smell me. I just pretend to smell him back. It tells him I am part of his herd."

"How about you bond by shoveling what he leaves behind?" Charlie said. "I didn't sign up for this. If my father knew—"

"Stop talking about your father. He's not here. I come from Toronto too. I recognize your family name. I know the area where you live and about the mansions behind the gates. My advice, whether you want it or not, is that in a platoon, it doesn't matter where you came from or how many connections your father has. Respect out here is earned."

"Didn't you hear me? I said no thanks to your stupid advice."

"Over here," Lance continued, "you can prove that you deserve respect for who you are, not who your family is. It's what we're doing as Canadian soldiers. Earning respect. Become one of us, and you'll get that respect."

"Finished?" Charlie asked.

Lance moved around to the side of Coal Dust and checked the saddle to make sure it was secure. He tugged the blanket beneath the saddle, more out of habit than anything. Lance always took care of his horse.

"If you don't want to talk, then yeah, I'm finished."

"Easy for you to give advice. You get to ride a horse. I clean up behind it."

Lance didn't bother pointing out to Charlie that he was about to ride Coal Dust on a scouting mission to confirm the location of an enemy machine gun nest, putting himself and his horse at risk.

After all, it didn't appear that Charlie thought about anyone but himself.

—•—

Before the war, Lance Wesley had been a traffic policeman in Toronto, and each day he'd spent hours on a horse, its hooves clattering the cobblestone at busy intersections.

He knew and appreciated the loyalty that a horse can have for a human. An understanding of the horse began with knowing that it was primarily a herd animal. When a horse showed teeth, it was showing that it was a herbivore, not a predator. Just like humans smiled to show they weren't a threat.

As large herd animals that lived off grasses, horses were built to detect the slightest of dangers from approaching predators. Of any land animals, horses had the largest eyes, and fully a third of their brains were devoted to vision. With eyes on the sides of their heads, they lacked the depth perception of dogs and cats and humans, for example, but they had amazing peripheral vision. In fact, they could almost see for a full 360 degrees, with small blind spots only directly behind and directly in front of them. Lance knew that because of those blind spots horses step to the side to see things behind them. He knew they backed up to lower their heads to see things in front. That was part of the natural rhythm of a horse, and Lance always gave rein to Coal Dust for that.

Lance could read a horse's emotions by the position of its ears. Laid back, the ears showed that the horse was in pain or afraid or ready to be aggressive.

But what Lance marveled at the most each time he rode Coal Dust was the superb design of the animal's legs. Coal Dust could walk, trot, canter or gallop on nearly any kind of terrain. The upper part of his leg held the bulk of the muscle, while the thin lower part was a springboard. All of it was supported by a complicated arrangement of ligaments and joint capsules. Horses' legs were flexible and long and powerful, capable of carrying a heavy load at amazing speeds. But horses' legs were also delicate. If broken, a horse's shattered leg would be impossible to repair.

That's why Lance feared for Coal Dust each time they went on a scouting mission.

A broken leg would mean death for his incredible companion.

—·—

Five other soldiers from various platoons rode with Lance. The weather for their mission was pleasant and balmy. Too often storms brought in the rain and cold that made life so miserable for the soldiers in the trenches. But today, Lance could pretend he was on a peaceful ride in the country.

Except it did not look like any countryside he had ever seen before.

The ground was pocked with craters from the huge shells that the opposing armies flung at each other from distances measured in miles. These craters had filled with water. Some craters were so deep that the mud walls were a treacherous, almost impossible to climb wall for anyone unfortunate enough to fall to the bottom.

Worse, however, were the unexploded shells, waiting for an unaware soldier or horse to trigger an explosion. All six riders moved carefully through the area.

Their destination was a hill on the horizon. From there, they hoped to map a hillside with the details that could not be seen from blimps above.

Then Lance heard the dreaded whistling sound. An incoming shell. Had the enemy spotted them and aimed for them? Or was it a random shot? The answer didn't matter, because the danger was the same either way.

"Scatter!" Lance yelled. His warning wasn't needed. All the cavalrymen were experienced and had already spurred their horses into motion.

Nobody could guess where the shell might land, so avoiding the explosion was a matter of luck. What did matter was getting all the horses as far apart as possible so that the shell wouldn't destroy all of them with a single horrible punch.

To Lance, it seemed to happen in slow, cartwheeling motion. With a thunderous roar, the earth rose beneath him and Coal

Dust. Lance's world went silent, his hearing temporarily destroyed in that moment. Yet his vision remained, and the sky went topsy-turvy as he was flung into the air.

Had he landed flat, the impact would have broken his ribs and injured him beyond repair.

Instead, Lance landed on the slippery slope of a crater and rolled and rolled. There was a snap of pain in his leg that fired a flash of white through his vision. And, finally, all movement stopped.

—•—

It took Lance a few minutes to stop his dizziness, and then he became fully aware that the lower part of his body was in water, the water at the bottom of the crater.

Ignoring the pain in his leg, Lance tried to crawl up the slope. It was too slick. He slid back, deeper in the water after than he had been before. If he tried it again, he might fall all the way into the water and drown.

If he could stand, perhaps . . .

He gasped as he placed the slightest of weight on his knees. His left leg. Broken. Maybe in one or two places.

It was an eerie fog of silence for Lance.

He tried to stay calm as he assessed his situation. It was a thirty-foot climb up a slope of greasy mud. If he had a rifle or even a bayonet, he could use it to stab deep into the mud and try to pull his body up. But even with two good legs, without a tool of any kind, it was hopeless.

He began to realize it had not been good fortune that stopped him from rolling all the way into the water to drown, and instead, it had only delayed what was ahead. Long hours, waiting for the end.

In came another shell. Because the pressure wave of air from the first one had instantly shattered his eardrums, Lance didn't hear the thunder of the next exploding shell. But he felt the vibrations in his ribs. If any of the other cavalry had survived, they would be long gone. Even if one of the soldiers had decided to stay to search for Lance, they wouldn't have seen him at the bottom of the crater. They'd assume his fate had been the worst. Missing in action.

Lance groaned. His sorrow was for the family he'd leave behind. And for Coal Dust. Such a noble animal had not deserved to die.

Then he wondered.

What if . . .

No. He told himself he shouldn't fool himself with hope. Even if Coal Dust had survived, the shell would have sent him running in panic. He would have stayed with the herd and galloped away with any surviving cavalry.

Yet . . .

Would there be any harm trying the only thing that could save him, even if it was a one-in-a-thousand chance?

Lance licked the mud from his fingers, and spit the mud back onto the slope of the crater.

When his fingers were clean, he stuck them in his mouth and whistled as loud as he could.

He couldn't even tell if it made noise, but he did it again and again. He craned his head upward, and then blinked in disbelief.

There, outlined against the lip of the crater above him, was Coal Dust.

—•—

Lance waited for the men who would carry him on a stretcher through the miles of trenches back to a hospital. He sat against the barn wall, his broken leg splinted in front of him. His hearing had still not returned. Doctors had promised it might come back in a day or two.

Beside him, with a pencil, Lieutenant Norman scratched out words on a notepad and held it front of Lance Wesley's face.

Keep going. What happened next?

Lance felt like he was still in a dream, partly because he'd been given morphine to take away the worst of his pain. Medics knew it was a dangerous painkiller because it could become addictive, and they had given him only a small dosage. So Lance was capable of conversation, even if it was writing and listening on one side by Lieutenant Norman and reading and speaking on Lance's side.

"That magnificent animal slowly stepped toward me," Lance told Lieutenant Norman. Lance's own words were a dull hum because he couldn't even hear what he was saying. Lance had to stop because tears began to flow down his cheeks and his throat was choked with gratitude. What courage that had taken for Coal Dust to return.

The other cavalrymen had reported that Coal Dust had been thrown onto his side but scrambled to his feet and bolted. But then Coal Dust had stopped as they goaded their own horses away from the danger.

"Even when a third shell landed, he didn't leave me." With four legs instead of two, Coal Dust could navigate the slope, even though the horse's feet went a full foot into the mud with each step. "And when he was close enough, he dropped his head so I could grab the reins."

Lance grinned through his tears. "Then he dragged me out, stepping backward slowly until we were clear of the crater.

He let me pull myself up into the saddle and then we were off and back here. I can't remember much of the ride, to be honest, because my leg hurt so bad. He knew exactly how to bring me home. He's fine, right? Coal Dust?"

Lieutenant Norman scratched again on the pad. *Jake is taking good care of him. Every single man in the platoon has spent time with Coal Dust telling him what a hero he is.*

"Thanks, sir." Lance had to trust that the words were coming out in the way he intended to say them because of his damaged eardrums.

You'll be headed back to Canada, Lieutenant Norman wrote. *Soldiers come back after a leg has healed, but if you're permanently deaf, you have a ticket out of the war.*

"You're wrong, sir," Lance said. "I'm not deaf. My hearing is perfect. Please tell them that at headquarters."

Lieutenant Norman didn't need to scratch out his question. It was obvious on his face as he stared at Lance. Why was Lance telling a lie?

"I can't leave Coal Dust, sir," Lance explained. "I hope you understand that."

Lieutenant Norman lifted the pad and wrote. He showed it to Lance, with a sad shake of his head. *A deaf soldier in a war zone puts all the other soldiers in danger. I can't let you return to the platoon .*

"I know that, sir," Lance said. "But can you make sure I'm able to stay behind the lines and take care of Coal Dust? Someone has to shovel, and I'll be happy to do it for the rest of the war."

WARRIOR

THE INSPIRATION BEHIND THE STORY OF
COAL DUST

The Victoria Cross is one of the highest medals of honor to be awarded to a soldier, and in the animal world, an equivalent award is called the Dickin Medal, recognized as the ultimate award an animal can achieve while serving in war.

A horse named Warrior received that medal for his bravery during World War One. Warrior served for the entire war, surviving machine gun attacks, falling shells and twice being trapped under burning beams in his stables.

Despite a horse's natural instinct to shy away from noise and explosions, Warrior never failed in charges against the enemy, and his presence was an inspiration to all the soldiers who fought alongside this magnificent animal.

FIRST NATIONS INVOLVEMENT IN WORLD WAR ONE

In the annual 1919 report from the Department of Indian Affairs, it was revealed that more than four thousand Aboriginals enlisted for service during the war. This is a staggering

percentage—it means that more than one out of every three First Nations men of military age volunteered for service, and according to the report, "the percentage of enlistments among the Indians is fully equal to that among other sections of the community, and indeed far above the average in a number of instances." In one community, for example, the Head of the Lake Band in British Columbia, every male member between the ages of twenty and twenty-five enlisted.

This number did not include those who identified as Aboriginals but were not registered as such, nor did it include Métis or Inuit, so the statistics do not account for an even greater number of volunteers from First Nations communities across Canada. Many of these soldiers did not speak English but were determined to help the war effort despite the added difficulties of a language barrier. Often their communities rallied behind them, raising money and sending supplies to help the war effort.

CAVALRY HORSES

At the beginning of World War One, cavalry units were used to attack enemy soldiers. However, the same reasons that led to trench warfare led to a more limited use of the cavalry—the modern machine gun and artillery fire, and the rolls of barbed wire meant to slow down soldiers.

While the British continued with some horseback charges on the enemy throughout the entire war, horses mostly served the soldiers in scouting and pulling artillery, supply and ambulance wagons.

Horses faced difficult conditions during the war. Like soldiers, they could be killed by artillery fire and poison gas. Because of the weather and lack of shelter, they also faced skin diseases and malnutrition.

It is estimated that on both sides of the war, over 8 million horses died during battles. Horses were so important to the war effort that in 1917, some officers considered the loss of a horse in battle to be as devastating as the loss of a soldier.

On March 30, 1918, the Germans began their final major battle, and the Canadian Cavalry Brigade played a vital role in halting the German attack. Although the larger German force was supported by machine gun fire, the Canadian cavalry charged. This brave action led to surrender by the German soldiers, but at great cost: only a quarter of the soldiers and horses survived the battle.

Jake watched Thomas Northstar sprinkle water over some slugs on his empty breakfast plate.

"Back on our farm," Jake said, "my mother hated what slugs did in her garden. She sprinkled salt on them."

"She did not need them to someday save her life," Thomas said. "Do I have to make mention of this each morning?"

"I think the two of you are crazy," Charlie said. His eyes were closed and he was leaning against the sandbags of the trench wall. "Seriously crazy. I hate listening to your conversations. And I'm tired of watching you collect slugs, like it's some kind of medicine man thing. Crazy Indian."

"*Kiwitinohk achakos*," Jake said. "Thomas, did I get that right?"

"Not bad," Thomas said.

Charlie frowned as he looked back and forth between the two. "Itchy aching what?"

Thomas laughed.

"Kiwitinohk achakos," Jake said again. "It's his name. That's Cree for Northstar. Jake calls himself Cree, Charlie. Not Indian."

"Then he should call himself Crazy Cree," Charlie said. "Translate that, why don't you."

"No," Jake said. "He is North Star. A guiding light for all of us in times of darkness."

Jake looked at Thomas. "I'm proud I managed to say that with a straight face. Did I sound wise when I said it?"

"Keep trying," Thomas said. "Almost as wise as when I say it."

Charlie buried his head and groaned. "Why me? Isn't trench duty enough punishment?"

"It is my sincere advice that you consider fighting in a different war," Thomas said. "Until then, you are stuck with me. And with Jake. And our wonderful little friends here. Did you know that each morning I pull these slugs from my nose? That makes it very strong medicine, white man."

"Enough!" Charlie said. "Enough! You guys are not funny!"

"Yes we are." Jake snorted with laughter, but stopped when he saw Thomas lose his smile and focus on the slugs.

"After all these mornings, it may be time," Thomas said in a calm voice. "Look. They are beginning to curl. No need to cause alarm, but perhaps you should go to the periscope and warn Justin."

Thomas was correct. The slugs had begun to wriggle, no differently than if salt had been poured on them.

Jake moved along the trench. It was lined with walls of sandbags. Without sandbags, the dirt would collapse. In some places, tin sheets offered scant protection against rain. But the trenches were horrible places to live, and soldiers would sometimes sleep standing up.

He'd heard that the Germans had fancy trenches, some with underground rooms big enough to hold a piano, where officers were served fancy dinners by waiters. He didn't want to believe that. Not when he might go for days without a chance to eat anything hot.

Jake could walk without ducking, because the trench was deep enough to hide his helmet from enemy snipers on the other side of No Man's Land. Jake kept his rifle and his backpack with him. Those were orders. A soldier caught without his rifle or backpack faced severe punishment.

Jake reached the part of the trench where Justin Biggs stood in front of a tall and skinny square box that reached above the top edge of the trench. Biggs was looking at the mirror on the bottom of the box. It was angled at forty-five degrees. At the top of the box was another mirror with the opposite forty-five degree angle. It was the periscope that let them survey the enemy without exposing themselves to bullets.

"You have that special mask for Boomer, right?" Jake asked Justin. "If so, it may be time."

"I don't see anything," Justin said. "Check it out for yourself."

Justin moved over so that Jake could peek into the periscope.

Jake paused before looking into the periscope and said, "You know how much Boomer hates the mask. You'll need as much warning as possible to get it over his head. Why don't you find Boomer just in case. If Thomas Northstar says there's danger, chances are there is danger."

Justin went to find Boomer, and for the next few minutes, Jake stared into the mirrors of the periscope. He saw coils and coils of barbed wire in front of their own trench. He saw the flat surface of No Man's Land, the vegetation long since shredded by artillery.

Then he saw a low, greenish-yellow fog sliding toward their own trench.

Jake didn't hesitate. He pulled his bayonet from his rifle. He and all the platoon had been drilled on this again and again. Hanging from a sandbag near the periscope was a large empty brass shell case, about the size of his forearm. He began to clang the brass shell.

Up and down the trenches, other soldiers echoed that alarm on their own empty brass shells. The threat was silent and even deadlier than the huge explosives lobbed by the enemy. Alarm gongs began to ring, and it was official. Orders for every soldier to get into gas masks.

Jake scrambled to get into his backpack as he raced back to Thomas.

That fog was made of two deadly chemicals, phosgene and chlorine. The first time it had been used against the Allied forces, there had been little defense. Now, each soldier carried two gas masks in their backpacks.

A little ways down the trench, a solider named Robert Carter shouted, "Tomato! Tomato!"

In that instant, Jake's world tilted. A shell had made an almost direct hit on the trench, sending shock waves of air that knocked him onto his back.

He shook his head, trying to keep his senses.

The gas was approaching! Thomas struggled to his knees, right beside Jake.

"Thomas," Jake groaned. "Smoke helmet."

Both managed to get to their knees and pull their gas masks loose from backpacks. At best, it still took eighteen seconds to get everything in place. They knew this because Lieutenant Norman drilled them again and again, using a watch to time them.

Gas mask in hand, Jake saw that Robert Carter was completely still, with a huge gash in his arm that streamed blood.

How much time before the gas hit?

"Charlie!" Jake yelled. "Thomas! We need help!"

Jake didn't have to explain more than that. The unconscious

man needed a gas mask on his face. That made it all the more urgent: eighteen seconds to secure their own masks, then another eighteen or more seconds for the unconscious man's.

Jake forced himself not to panic. He took a deep breath, knowing if he rushed, he'd probably make a mistake and waste time. When everything was in place, he found himself peering through the two glass eyes of his mask and heard the sound of his breathing.

He turned his head to the unconscious man. That's when Jake saw Charlie run past him down the trenches. Away from the man who needed help.

Coward, Jake thought. But this wasn't the time to deal with it. The men who were down needed the gas masks. One deep breath of the poison and Robert Carter would not survive.

Jake stumbled toward the fallen man. Thomas joined him.

"You get his arm," Jake said. His voice echoed in his own ears. The mask muffled him and he had to yell to be heard. "I'll get the mask."

Jake slid Robert's gas mask over the man's head and put the flaps in place. Thomas took a short piece of rope and wrapped it around Robert's arm, above the wound. He tightened it with the tourniquet technique and the bleeding slowed. Then Thomas slapped a bandage over it, just as Robert started to come around.

Five seconds later, the green cloud rolled down into the trench.

Jake heard a yell from the platoon's telephone operator, William Kane. The yell was muffled by William's gas mask, but Jake still clearly heard the man's words.

"Our lines have been cut!"

No telephone communication with the rear trenches. It could only mean one thing.

The enemy was preparing to attack over the top of the trenches.

Jake was still on his knees in the mud, beside Robert Carter.

Robert groaned and clutched at Jake. "You have to find Tomato. He needs his gas mask. Look in my pack."

Jake pawed through Robert's backpack, but the only other gas mask was Robert's spare.

"Not here," Jake said.

Robert groaned from inside his mask. "Without him, we won't be able to warn rear quarters about the situation. You have to find him alive or all of us are done when the attack comes."

— • —

Most of the platoon soldiers were busy bringing up extra ammunition to the machine guns to prepare for the attack. In the chaos, Jake couldn't find Lieutenant Norman. If he had been a British soldier, leaving his position without permission might have led to punishment.

But Lieutenant Norman, like all the Canadian officers, had been given orders from the very top and told to pass it down to his men. In battle situations, all the soldiers were told to think for themselves. Follow the battle plan if possible, but when situations changed, react accordingly.

Jake hurried down the trench to find the border collie named Tomato. With the greenish gas sinking to the bottom of the trenches, Jake had little hope that Tomato was still alive, but he had promised Robert he would search.

Mud sucked at Jake's boots. It was even more difficult to walk because the mask made it seem like he was looking through twin tunnels. He couldn't see out of the corner of his eye, and Jake's breathing was uncomfortable. The nose of the gas mask was treated with chemicals that neutralized the poisonous gas. He had to breathe through his nose to suck the outside air through those chemicals, and then exhale through a tube in his mouth. The tube was airtight to keep the poison gas from getting inside.

The helmet was good for about five hours before the protection of the chemicals in the nose wore out. That's why every soldier carried two helmets. Jake reminded himself of the steps he'd practiced. To replace the helmet, you had to hold your breath while you took off the first helmet.

Jake pushed past soldiers who were standing on benches along the sandbagged walls.

"Tomato," Jake said. "Seen him?"

A soldier had a stick with a helmet on top. He pushed the helmet above the trench. About a second later, a bullet spun the helmet in a circle. The soldier brought the helmet down and peered at it through the glass circles of his gas mask.

"Tomato," Jake repeated. "Seen him?"

"Last I saw him was with Freddy." The soldier pushed his finger through the bullet hole in the steel helmet. "Don't know why we have to wear one. Don't seem to do much good, does it?"

Without answering, Jake pushed on toward Freddy. He expected he would find Tomato, just not alive. Animals didn't deserve what the gas did to them. Neither, Jake thought, did humans.

Jake saw Charlie first. It wasn't easy to recognize other men when you were wearing gas masks. But the uniform on Charlie's left shoulder had a rip on it so Jake knew who it was.

Jake felt his anger flare. Bad enough to be in the trenches under a gas attack with the enemy about to rush them. But when you couldn't depend on a fellow soldier, that was the worst.

He grabbed Charlie's shoulder and spun Charlie toward him.

"You," Jake yelled. The sound hurt his own ears because much of his voice seemed trapped in the gas mask. "We needed you."

"I know you did," Charlie said. "That's why I went running. Robert was down and couldn't help Tomato."

Charlie pointed a little farther down the trench. Tomato stood, tail wagging at the sound of his name.

He was alive. Wearing the special gas mask that had been designed for a dog's head. The one that Charlie had pulled from Robert's backpack before running down the trench to save Tomato.

That's what Canadian soldiers did. Even when they didn't like each other. When necessary, they reacted to the situation and made decisions without waiting for orders.

Charlie had saved Tomato. But it still didn't mean the platoon would get help in time. The rest would depend on Tomato.

—·—

Because the trenches were so complex and the telephone technology was always breaking down or being sabotaged, commanders needed a reliable field communication system.

Human runners were a large target, weighed down by heavy, wet uniforms and mud-caked boots. During artillery fire, there was too great a chance of injury.

Roads were mud bogs, and even when logs were rolled onto the mud to support vehicles, they were easy targets to be shot, and broke down frequently.

That's what made Tomato so valuable to the platoon.

Tomato was a happy-go-lucky border collie. He had come

to the platoon with his name, given to him because as a puppy, he'd sneaked into a kitchen and eaten so many stewed tomatoes that he'd been sick for a day.

In a sense, he was just an ordinary dog. But that's only because it's too easy to think of dogs as ordinary.

In another sense, he was extraordinary because of how he had been trained. Pigeons were wonderful for delivering messages to a fixed base but too often would be shot down or attacked by hawks. The shifting balance of battles often demanded communication between officers separated by miles of trenches, officers who were constantly changing positions.

For that, the soldiers needed the most elite soldier dog of the front. A liaison dog like Tomato.

Many dogs were trained as messengers, and operated much like pigeons, with a homing instinct. The dog could deliver a message from anywhere in the trenches back to headquarters.

But it took double the training and much more intelligence for a dog to learn to go between two handlers who could be anywhere in the trenches at any time. Tomato had to use all of his smelling skills, guessing skills and running skills to track down his second handler in the maze of trenches when Robert Carter gave him the correct command.

Now, against odds that no human could overcome, Tomato needed to reach his second handler with the information about the gas attack.

—•—

"He's ready," Robert said. Robert sat with his back against the sandbags of the trench, his injured arm bandaged and in a sling against his side. Lieutenant Norman had already marched down the trench, a grim look on his face, leaving behind the messages that were in a canister on a collar around Tomato's neck.

In the fog of greenish gas that surrounded them, Tomato looked like a creature from another world. The gas mask fitted for his canine skull gave him bulging eyes like a giant fly.

"Deliver!" Robert said, his voice muffled by the gas mask. This meant for Tomato to go directly back to rear quarters and look for the other handler.

Tomato stayed in place, whining.

"Deliver!" Robert said again.

Tomato pawed the ground.

"What's the problem?" Charlie asked. "You heard Lieutenant Norman. Sooner than later the enemy is going to try to make it over the top. We need more men brought up the line."

Jake said, "It sounds like the dog is worried about Robert."

For all of them, it almost sounded like they were underwater, with their voices trapped by the gas masks that kept them alive.

"It's just a dog," Charlie said. "It's not that smart."

"Let Tomato see your face," Thomas told Robert. "Let him see your eyes as you tell him you are not seriously hurt."

"That's stupid," Charlie said. "Take off the smoke helmet?"

Jake wanted to punch Charlie. He reminded himself that Charlie had done some remarkably quick thinking to save Tomato.

"You are a creature of the city, and you experience animals by the different spices you use on them as you eat," Thomas said to Charlie. "I am not of the city and have lived in the woods my entire life and understand nature. I watch slugs to learn when poison gas approaches."

Jake said to Robert, "Are you going to listen to Charlie or to Thomas?"

"I'll hold my breath long enough for you to take off the

mask," Robert said. "Jake, help me put it back on again after Tomato sees that I'm all right."

Jake hesitated. He knew if he wasn't fast enough getting the mask in place, the poison would do fatal damage to Robert.

"Do it!" Robert said.

Jake lifted the cloth of Robert's gas mask away from his neck where Robert, like each soldier, had tucked it into his collar. Jake lifted the mask and Robert exposed his face to Tomato and nodded and smiled.

The dog bolted down the trench, dodging soldiers with huge leaps of confidence.

Jake pulled the mask down in position, counting the seconds. He didn't get higher than nineteen, and it was in place.

With his uninjured hand, Robert gave Jake a thumbs-up.

"Huh," Thomas said in a muffled voice. "It actually worked. I didn't know I was that smart."

—•—

Not only was Tomato one of the smartest dogs among all the breeds, he was fast.

In a straight stretch, a greyhound could beat him for a short distance, going in short bursts of seventy kilometers (43 mi.) an hour. But ask the greyhound to twist and turn as if it were chasing sheep, and Tomato would dust it.

Tomato leaped over or ducked under obstacles and made sharp turns at the corners of trenches with incredible agility. He was unencumbered by any weight, only the smoke mask that made him breathe hard.

Without smell to guide him, he relied on his memories of the maze. At each intersection he would choose the correct turn without hesitation.

Then adaptive instinct told him a shorter route was to go up and over a trench wall and dash through the mud. He jumped up the sandbags and out of the trench, exposed to the enemy. With great leaps, he barely touched down and bounced forward again, dodging from one side to another to avoid craters and unexploded shells. He leaped over curls of barbed wire in one place, then scraped beneath those curls when the depth was too great to jump.

He was an impossible target for snipers, a blur of black and white, boundless energy, focused on one thing.

Deliver the message.

—•—

With waves of enemy soldiers trying to dash across No Man's Land in the wake of the poison gas, Jake helped man a machine gun turret. He fed clips of bullets into the weapon for the shooter, keeping his head down, focused on one thing.

Fight.

But something bounced off his gas mask, and there was a loud crack. Dryness hit his throat. It felt like a large snake had curled around his body to squeeze his lungs. He began to get dizzy, and it seemed like soldiers around him were floating in the air.

He toppled into the mud. It felt like scorpions were jabbing his skin. He clawed at his gas mask. Then everything went black.

But not for long. When he woke in the shadows at the bottom of the trench, Thomas was removing his gas mask.

"It's a good thing you had your second one nearby," Thomas said. Thomas wasn't wearing his own gas mask. "Even so, we thought you were gone."

Jake squinted. "What's that I hear?"

Thomas squinted back, puzzled. "Nothing."

Jake wanted to throw up, but the cool, fresh air revived him. "Exactly. Nothing. No machine guns. No artillery shells. I love the sound of silence. That attack didn't last long."

"Jake," Thomas said, "you were out for two hours."

"What?" Jake tried to sit.

Thomas offered him water from a canteen. Jake sipped. His throat hurt as he swallowed.

"Two hours," Thomas repeated. "We managed to hold them off until a couple of platoons reached us. Tomato made it to the rear quarters in what everyone believes was record time."

"What happened? How did I get my second mask on?" Jake said.

"Thank Charlie," Thomas said. "He was the one who saw the hole in your mask when you fell. He ripped off your damaged mask, kept a hand over your mouth and nose so you couldn't breathe, then yelled for me to get the other mask in place. Even then, we did not know if it worked."

Thomas patted Jake's shoulder. "I am glad it did. Of anyone, it is you I like beating the most in chess."

"Glad I'm good for something," Jake said. "Robert Carter okay?"

"Getting patched up now. He'll be fine."

"And Tomato?" Jake asked.

"Call for him," Thomas said.

Jake gave a short yell. It was more like a croak, because Jake's throat still hurt. But it was enough.

Seconds later, Tomato was there in the trench, licking Jake's face.

"Hey," Jake laughed. "Cut that out. I've seen you lick yourself, and I don't like where your tongue has been."

SATAN OF VERDUN AND JACK

THE INSPIRATION BEHIND THE STORY OF

TOMATO

Jack's battalion was under such heavy fire that only reinforcements and more ammunition would save the soldiers. The soldier who sent the plucky Airedale terrier out with a message under his collar gave him simple instructions: "Good-bye, Jack. Go back, boy."

Jack's first obstacle was a deep swamp that kept him safe from bullets. But after he left the swamp, he was hit by shrapnel that broke his jaw, ripped his shoulder and splintered his leg. He dragged himself the last few miles until he reached his handler. Although Jack did not survive, he saved the battalion and earned a Victoria Cross for bravery.

One of the war's most brutal battles took place when the Germans laid siege to the French city of Verdun, which lasted from February 21 to December 18, 1916, one of the longest and most costly battles in human history.

A French garrison was trapped. With no remaining food or

ammunition, it appeared that there were only two choices: death or surrender. Then racing toward them came what looked like a monster with a massive  head and horrible strange eyes and wings on its back. Then the soldiers realized it was a dog named Satan, returning with a message to his handler.

The horrible strange eyes were the gas mask that Satan wore, and the two wings were wicker baskets on Satan's back, each holding a homing pigeon. The French soldiers wrote two duplicate messages, each with information about the location of the German guns. One pigeon did not make it, but the second pigeon delivered the message, and within minutes, French artillery managed to destroy the German guns and the French soldiers were saved.

GAS WARFARE

A major reason behind the eventual success at Vimy Ridge was the willingness of Canadian officers to discard military traditions that didn't make sense in the type of warfare that involved new weapons and tactics.

An early example of this happened at Ypres, Belgium, when Canadians were furious that British commanding officers dismissed warnings of almost certain gas attacks. By then, captured German soldiers had given specific details about gas cylinders ready and waiting to be used. Even after patrols confirmed these reports, the "feeling at the top was that the Germans would never be so ungentlemanly as to use gas against their enemies."

Yet on April 22, 1915, this is exactly what happened. During what was later described as the Second Battle of Ypres, the

Germans first shelled the Allied soldiers. Then, instead of attacking as usual, the Germans released chlorine gas that decimated two divisions of Allied soldiers across a 6.5 kilometer (4 mi.) stretch of the front.

This led to an arms race of chemical warfare. Gas masks were put into service as protection, and new, more deadly gases were developed. Phosgene came next, a devious gas that caused much less coughing, which meant soldiers inhaled more of it.

Introduced in 1917, mustard gas was considered the most deadly, causing not only skin blisters, but blisters inside the lungs. It was so deadly that it remained in the soil for weeks afterward, making capture of the infected trenches very dangerous.

All told, it is estimated that the Germans used 62,000 metric tonnes (68,000 tn.) of gas, while the French used barely half that and the British even less.

DIFFICULTY OF MOVEMENT IN THE TRENCHES

With their strategy of attacking first and gaining as much ground as possible, the Germans took over a great deal of territory in France and Belgium. But as the British and French troops rallied, it became obvious to the Germans that they needed to find a way to defend the land that they had taken.

The Germans then dug the first trenches, and soon the equally matched armies were in a race to the sea, trying to outflank the trenches of the other army. It ended with two opposing trench lines that ran from the North Sea down to the border of Switzerland.

The Germans had the advantage because they had been the first to dig in and they took the upper ground. The British, French and Canadian troops had no choice but to dig in soil that was often only a couple of feet above sea level.

This led to frequent flooding and trenches that were constantly full of water and mud, which made moving around difficult. To add to that difficulty, trenches were dug in a zigzag pattern. If trenches were straight, an invading enemy would be able to fire down the entire length.

MESSENGER DOGS IN WORLD WAR ONE

Homing pigeons were the fastest way to deliver messages from the trenches. But homing pigeons were only a one-way system—from the front lines to headquarters. Messenger dogs could travel between two handlers. When it was impossible to communicate via telephone, a dog could run through and between trenches at much greater speeds than a human messenger, choosing the most efficient route to deliver important messages as quickly as possible. Despite the difficult conditions, messenger dogs could sometimes cover 5 kilometers (3 mi.) in only fifteen minutes.

Most messenger dogs were taught to always return to a handler, known as a keeper. When working, the keeper and his dog would first go to headquarters. Then the dog would be taken by another soldier to the front. When told to return to its keeper, the dog would use its natural intelligence and homing instinct to deliver the message attached to its collar.

Messenger dogs had two advantages over pigeons. The first was that homing pigeons were trained to return only to where they had been born. The messenger dog could return to a variety of locations, dependent only on where it had last been with its keeper.

This led to the second advantage: the one-way delivery could be reversed. A keeper and his dog would go the front, and then the dog would be taken to headquarters at the rear so that front-line officers could receive new instructions from headquarters.

Some messenger dogs were even trained to go back and forth between two keepers, so that during crucial times of battle, the same dog could take messages back and forth. This was much more dangerous for the dog, however, as it had to double its time in the danger zones.

"If you want, I'll break this candle in half so that you can use the other half," Jake said to Thomas.

The platoon was on leave from the front lines. Duties were finished for the morning, and all the soldiers were gathered beneath trees at the edge of a French village. Most of them, like Jake, had pulled off their shirts. Most of them, like Jake, were running a lit candle below the seams of those shirts. It had been days in the filth of the trenches, and days since any had been able to wash with water, so this was the next best thing.

"Your way takes too long," Thomas said. "I notice that you burn the threads if the flame gets too close. Then you have holes in your shirt. I have decided to try something else."

A few feet away, Lieutenant Norman used a long-handled wooden spoon to reach over his shoulder and scratch his back. His shirt was on a branch beside him. Lieutenant Norman had his eyes closed and sighed with satisfaction as he rubbed the spoon on his skin.

"Charlie," Thomas said, "would you do me a favor?"

Charlie didn't look up from running a candle flame along the seams of his own shirt. "I'm busy."

"He's not the kind of guy who does favors," Jake said. "Haven't you figured that out?"

"Charlie," Thomas said, "if you will do me a favor, I will give you chocolate when the mail gets here."

Charlie looked up and frowned. "I'd sure like to know why you get so many more packages in the mail than anyone else around here."

Thomas said, "You are not interested in doing me a favor for chocolate?"

"Then it wouldn't be a favor," Charlie said. "It would be a deal."

"Then let us make the deal," Thomas said. "Hold my shirt for me. And in exchange I will give you chocolate the next time a package comes in the mail."

"In my mansion in Toronto," Charlie said, "I wouldn't have to stoop this low for chocolate. I'd snap my fingers and a maid would bring me some."

"Does this look like Toronto to you?" Jake asked.

Charlie turned to Thomas, "Give me the shirt."

Charlie stood. Thomas handed Charlie the shirt.

"Hold it away from you," Thomas said. "I don't want you to get hurt."

"Hurt?"

Thomas picked up a shovel that was leaning against a tree. He whacked the shirt with the shovel blade, like he was beating a rug. Black dots sprayed everywhere from his shirt.

"Hey!" Charlie shouted. Charlie dropped the shirt and slapped himself as the black dots ran all across his skin. "Now I've got *your* lice."

"As usual, I have impressed myself," Thomas said to Jake. "I must have knocked off a couple hundred of them with just one swing. How long will it take you to get that many with a candle?"

"I like the sound when the flame makes them pop," Jake said. "It's the only revenge I can take against these lice."

"Hey," Charlie said to Thomas. "Didn't you hear me? *Your* lice are on *my* body."

"At least you are popular with something," Jake said.

"If this was Toronto," Charlie began, "you would see—"

"Look around for the streetcars," Jake interrupted. "Oh, right. There are none. It's safe to cross the road. Why? Because this isn't Toronto. And your mommy isn't here to kiss all your boo-boos better."

Charlie took two steps toward Jake. "I've had enough from you."

Lieutenant Norman spoke. "Boys, save the fighting for the enemy."

"He started it," Charlie said.

Lieutenant Norman laughed. "You sound like children. Except you're going to have to get along for at least one afternoon because I've got orders for you three to join me in a meeting with Major McNaughton as soon as a car arrives to take us to his headquarters."

"Major McNaughton?" Charlie said, almost gasping. "*The* Major McNaughton?"

"He puts his legs in his pants one at a time like the rest of us," Lieutenant Norman said. "Even so, I suppose the three of you should try to clean up as best as possible. Whatever it is, it must be important."

—•—

"It's that building down the street," the driver said. "The small house with the red door. You can walk the rest of the way."

It had been a half hour ride in the open-roofed car, bumping along cobblestone roads through the French countryside to reach the large village. They had not driven away from the front line of trenches, but alongside it, so in the distance they could still hear the booming of artillery shells.

Lieutenant Norman stepped out first, followed by Jake, Charlie and Thomas. Clouds threatened rain, but so far it was dry.

Jake scratched a few times. It was impossible to get all of the lice out of a uniform.

Charlie scratched too, and every time he did, he gave Thomas a dirty look.

They headed toward the building, with soldiers and officers walking in small groups around them in both directions. A small dog began to follow them. It had floppy ears, wiry fur and a bearded muzzle.

"Who is this?" Jake said, leaning down to scratch the dog's ears.

"Do not do that," Thomas said. "It will follow you forever."

The dog trotted over to Thomas and whined.

"Go away," Thomas said. "I will not scratch your head. You look like a scruffy British officer. Like the one on the street ahead of us."

The dog stayed right at Thomas's heels.

"Grr," Thomas said. The dog stopped and lifted a paw.

"Grr," Thomas said and kept walking. It stayed close to him.

Halfway down the street, that officer in British uniform stopped them.

The dog growled. Thomas put his hand on the dog and it stopped growling.

"I didn't see a salute from any of you," the British officer said. He had a haughty British accent. His uniform was pressed and perfectly clean. His mustache was trimmed and he looked at them through round spectacles.

Lieutenant Norman stared at the British officer. Lieutenant Norman's shoulders straightened. Jake had seen that

86

posture before. It meant that he was angry. It didn't happen too often, but when it did, the men of the platoon listened carefully to anything he said.

"I said I didn't see a salute from any of you," the British officer repeated.

Lieutenant Norman said, "Then your glasses provide you with excellent vision. Thanks for sharing your observation with us."

Jake wanted to laugh but knew this wasn't the time.

"By your stripes, I see you are a lieutenant," the British officer said to Lieutenant Norman. "And by the looks of your uniform, you don't spend much time this far behind the line."

"Not much time at all," Lieutenant Norman said.

"Not much time at all, *sir.*"

"Thank you," Lieutenant Norman said. "But by your stripes, it looks like you outrank me. No need to call me sir."

The British officer's face darkened. "What I *meant* was you forgot to add 'sir' to your answer. As in, not much time at all, *sir.*"

Lieutenant Norman said nothing.

"Well?"

"Well, thanks for the advice," Lieutenant Norman said. "So if you don't mind, the boys and I have a meeting just down the street with Major McNaughton."

"Thanks for the advice, *sir,*" the officer said. "You Canadians need to learn to show respect for uniforms. What I expect is that you salute every superior officer you see as you walk down this street."

"Then it's a good thing I'm in the Canadian army," Lieutenant Norman said. "Not the British army. I'll answer to my own officers, not to you or any other British officers or French. If I see a Canadian officer, I'll be sure to salute."

"In any army, rules must be followed. The three men with you are clearly ranked no higher than privates. Not one stripe between the three of them."

"That's not correct," Lieutenant Norman said.

"Of course it is. I don't see a single stripe."

"You said not one stripe 'between' the three of them," Lieutenant Norman said. "You only use the word 'between' when there are two. 'Among' is for three or more. I only point this out because it appears you are concerned about being proper. I believe the correct way to say it is 'not one stripe *among* the three of them.' Thomas, wouldn't you agree?"

"Yes, *sir*," Thomas said. "Bad grammar is not becoming of an officer at all."

The British officer shifted his gaze to stare at Thomas. The British officer looked down at the moccasins Thomas wore.

"A savage no less," the British officer said in a snooty voice. "The Canadian army has even lower standards than I could imagine."

He pointed downward at Thomas's moccasins and sneered. "What are *those*?"

"Feet," Thomas said. "It is something that all savages are taught by their parents at a young age. I am sad that it appears British parents do not do the same for their own children."

"Tell him about your toes," Charlie said to Thomas. "He should know that feet have toes."

"Why thank you," Thomas said to Charlie. Thomas turned back to the British officer. "I have five toes on each foot. It is such a help when I need to count things and I run out of fingers."

The British officer swallowed a few times, as if trying not to explode.

"You have pushed me too far," the British officer finally said to Lieutenant Norman. "It is not permissible for an officer to walk in public with men who are not officers. Do something about this immediately. No man with stripes shall be seen in social conversation with a private."

"Jake," Lieutenant Norman said. "How about lending me your knife."

"Yes, *sir.*" Jake emphasized the 'sir' like Thomas had, just to make a point to the British officer. Jake took his knife out of the sheath on his belt. He flipped it so that when he gave it to Lieutenant Norman, he was offering the handle, not the blade.

"Thank you," Lieutenant Norman said.

"Yes, sir," Jake said. Jake saluted Lieutenant Norman and enjoyed seeing the sour look that crossed the British officer's face because of the salute.

Lieutenant Norman used his free hand to reach across his shoulder and tug at the stripes on his sleeve. With the knife hand, he cut the stripes off his uniform. He handed the stripes to the British officer.

"Problem solved," Lieutenant Norman said. "Stripes gone, I can talk to my men. Now if you'll step aside, the four of us must be on our way."

—•—

As they arrived at the house with the red door, the British officer pushed his way in front of them and stomped down the hallway to Major McNaughton's office.

"Wait until I have a word with your senior officer," the British officer said over his shoulder to the four of them. "Then we shall see about proper discipline."

"Stay out here," Thomas told the dog. "Better yet, go away while we are inside."

The four of them entered the house. They saw that a soldier stood at the doorway to Major McNaughton's office.

"Stand aside," the British officer barked.

"I think—"

"You do not think," the British officer said. "That is not your job. Your job is to obey without question. What is wrong with the Canadian army? Now stand aside."

The soldier stepped away, and the British officer pushed open the door and stepped into Major McNaughton's office.

Jake clearly heard a roar. To him, it sounded like a lion.

Jake also heard a scream. To him, it sounded like a British officer.

The soldier at the doorway shrugged and looked at Lieutenant Norman, Jake, Charlie and Thomas. "I tried telling him."

They stood at the doorway and peered inside.

The office did not look the way Jake had expected. Cartons were heaped in piles. Metal chairs leaned against the far wall. The desk in the center of the room was not a desk. Instead, it was a sheet of board placed on top of stacked packing cases.

Jake did not see Major McNaughton.

Jake did see the British officer, standing on top of Major McNaughton's makeshift desk.

Jake also saw a lion cub. It was the size of a large dog. It stood on its hind legs as it swiped at the British officer's legs with its front paws. It roared again. The British officer screamed again.

"Shoot this thing!" the British officer screamed.

Lieutenant Norman saluted the lion cub.

"Not salute!" the British officer screamed. "Shoot!"

Thomas stepped forward. The lion cub turned and crouched and roared at Thomas.

Thomas said in a calm voice, "He will not taste good, my little friend. Leave the officer be."

The lion cub tilted his head and roared again.

"You give me no choice," Thomas said. "Remember, I wanted us to be civil."

He pointed at the lion and took a step closer and said, "*Piyatuk kitha Pi nasin kwayask kowikasin chipatahotani.*"

The lion cub whimpered, backed away and hid under the desk.

"As usual," Thomas said, dusting his hands, "I am nothing but impressive."

"Need help down from the desk, sir?" Lieutenant Norman asked the British officer.

"I want nothing to do with any of you! Canadians are crazy."

The British officer slid down from the desk and tried to keep his dignity as he marched past them. "Crazy! I now understand why the Germans are terrified of you."

The lion cub padded over and Jake began scratching the cub's head.

"Stand at ease," Lieutenant Norman said. "When Major McNaughton gets here, we should look like soldiers."

From down the hallway, they could hear a loud, angry voice. It sounded like a one-sided conversation. It was the British officer. Yelling.

Then came a reply with a Canadian accent. "What a shame. Anything else then?"

Silence.

"What was it you said to the lion?" Charlie asked Thomas. "It sounded a lot like something you say to me sometimes."

"It is of no matter," Thomas said. "Notice, however, that the lion was smart enough to pay attention. Perhaps you should do the same when I say those words to you."

From behind them came a voice. "Welcome to Canadian Field Artillery. Lieutenant Norman, correct?"

The four of them turned. The man in the doorway had dark, piercing eyes and shaggy hair and an equally shaggy mustache. His uniform seemed to be nothing but stripes.

"Andy McNaughton," the man said.

All four saluted.

"Please," Major McNaughton said. "No need for that here. Introduce yourselves."

As they gave Major McNaughton their names, the lion cub came out from under the desk. Major McNaughton scratched behind its ears.

"This is Leo," Major McNaughton said. "My staff captain was in Paris a few weeks ago and heard that the zoo was going to execute animals because of a shortage of rations. He rescued this fine animal, and I've become very fond of Leo. But usually he attacks anyone who enters my office without me. I'm surprised he didn't send you running."

"Thomas and Leo had a conversation," Lieutenant Norman said. "Leo understands Cree, it seems."

"Excellent," Major McNaughton said. "Now, you're probably wondering why I've asked the four of you to meet with me. Grab some chairs and let me get started."

—•—

"You are aware of the importance of Vimy Ridge," Major McNaughton began from his chair behind the desk. "So I won't waste time explaining why we badly need to remove the enemy from that vantage point. You're also aware that the British failed to take it, as did the French. You're probably *not* aware that at high levels the British and French have made it clear they don't expect the Canadians will be able do it. So I have a question. How badly would you like to prove them wrong?"

Major McNaughton put up a hand to stop any of the four from answering from their own chairs, a tight arc across from his desk.

"I know the answer because on my way in I had to listen to a British officer complain about how badly he'd been treated by a Canadian lieutenant and three privates. Apparently the Canadian lieutenant cut off his own stripes to make a point. Lieutenant Norman, I notice threads hanging from your sleeve and some missing stripes."

Major McNaughton leaned forward and opened his other hand and let the stripes fall on his desk. "I trust these are yours."

"I'm prepared to face the consequences," Lieutenant Norman said. "I want you to know that my men here did nothing wrong and I am fully to blame."

"Except that one of your men felt the need to suggest the officer's parents had failed to educate that officer about feet. And another of your men suggested the officer did not know that feet have toes or the number of toes per foot."

"My fault entirely," Lieutenant Norman said. "I set the example for them to follow. I should have disciplined them immediately, but instead allowed it to continue."

"Because you don't think that officers are superior to the men they lead."

"If you put it like that, yes. I lead my men, but we are equals. When someone suggests otherwise, I am not as polite as I should be. I will make no apology for that to the British officer."

"What about to me? Will you apologize to me?"

"I will accept full punishment."

"But not apologize."

"I will accept full punishment."

Major McNaughton grinned as he leaned back in his chair. "You are exactly the type of officer that we need and want. It's why our top officers refused to allow Canadian soldiers to be split up and put under British command."

Major McNaughton reached under his desk and scratched Leo's head again. "You know why I have a lion in my office?"

"To eat British officers?" Thomas asked.

Major McNaughton laughed. "That proves my point. There is no way a British private would dare speak like that in front of a major. And the fact that I find it funny proves something too, doesn't it."

The major leaned forward. "There are days I wouldn't mind if Leo took a good chunk out of a British, or a French, officer. But it's more than that. Leo is a mascot. Mascots improve morale and are as important to our soldiers as any other animal. There's a bear named Winnipeg that one of our soldiers brought over, and that animal is so gentle it brings a smile to everyone who meets it."

Major McNaughton snorted. "That can't be said about Leo, but when Leo sits beside me in my car, soldiers cheer as we pass them. They know I keep this lion exactly because the British and French repeatedly tell me that it's not how things are done in the army. Well, the way things are done in their armies hasn't exactly worked out every time. So Leo reminds them, and me, that I *am* going to do it differently. And I have the full support of General Byng."

Without warning, Major McNaughton stood. "I want the four of you to follow me, please. What I'd like to do next is not something that should happen in a room where the desk isn't even a desk."

Jake thought it said something, too, that Major McNaughton asked them instead of ordered them.

It was his first realization that, yes, the Canadians could actually do the impossible and take Vimy Ridge.

—·—

When all of them stepped outside, the scruffy dog moved straight to Thomas and whined and wagged its tail.

"Ahh," Major McNaughton said. "Your platoon has a mascot of its own. Wonderful. What's his name?"

"Colonel Scruffington," Charlie said when no one answered. "Scruffy, for short."

Lieutenant Norman cleared his throat. "Named after a British officer, of course."

"Of course," Major McNaughton said with a smile.

Scruffy followed as Major McNaughton led them to a garden behind the house that served as headquarters. It was well-tended, and Jake had to remind himself that he did not live in a world where *all* the ground was torn apart by artillery explosions. Someday, when the war was over, he could return to a world like this garden. It made him miss home.

Major McNaughton stopped them at the base of a large tree.

"To take Vimy," Major McNaughton said, "I want soldiers with the discipline of a well-trained pack of hounds. Soldiers who will find their own holes through the hedges. I'm not going to tell them where those holes are or how to get through them. I want soldiers who can find those holes themselves and get through those holes their own way. Soldiers who will never lose sight of the objective as they do it."

He gave a tight smile. "Those aren't my words. More or less, they come directly from General Byng himself. You do realize how different this is from the British and French approach. General Byng was furious to hear that six thousand French soldiers were commanded to attack enemy machine guns with bayonets and were not permitted to fire their own rifles until given the order to do so."

Major McNaughton paced away from them and back. "Lieutenant Norman, I have heard good things about your platoon. I want you to serve under me at Vimy Ridge as we prepare for a big push."

Lieutenant Norman took a deep breath of surprise. Then he grinned.

"It would be an honor," Lieutenant Norman said. "And with respect, sir, may I ask why you needed these men with me to make that request?"

"I didn't need them for that," Major McNaughton said. "I needed them for this."

Major McNaughton pulled an envelope out of his pocket.

"There was a recent gas attack and your platoon saved many men that day," Major McNaughton said. "These three men, I'm told, were exceptional under fire."

"They were," Lieutenant Norman answered. "I am very proud of them."

"You should be." Major McNaughton slid three medals out of the envelope. "They've each been awarded a Distinguished Conduct Medal. I'd prefer to pin it on their uniforms out here instead of in my office."

Major McNaughton paused when he got to Thomas. "There is one condition. You must tell me exactly what you said in Cree to Leo. The British officer said you sent the lion from a roar into a whimper, and trust me, I've never seen that happen before."

"I did not know he was your lion," Thomas said. "Otherwise I would never have made Leo that solemn promise."

"Which was?"

"Well . . . some words in Cree are difficult to translate."

"I'd like to know what you said."

Thomas spoke in a solemn voice. "I told him he would taste good after a little time on a stick over a campfire."

WINNIE AND A RESCUED LION CUB

THE INSPIRATION BEHIND THE STORY OF
LEO

Mascots played a very important role in soldiers' lives in the trenches. Pets like cats and dogs gave comfort and helped make life seem more normal while still serving a practical purpose. But all sorts of mascots became part of units throughout the entire war: monkeys, goats, pigs, donkeys, birds and even lizards.

For one Canadian unit, the adoption of a mascot occurred long before reaching the front. At a train stop in White River, Ontario, on his way to join the war, Canadian soldier Lieutenant Harry Colebourn saw a bear cub for sale for $20. He named it Winnipeg for his home city, and he took Winnipeg all the way to

Europe, where the bear became a mascot and pet for the Second Canadian Infantry Brigade Headquarters.

Lieutenant Colebourn intended to bring the bear back to the zoo in Winnipeg, so before going to France, he left the bear at the London Zoo for safekeeping. After the war, however, Winnie, as the bear was known, remained at the zoo, much loved for her gentleness and playfulness. A boy named Christopher Robin loved the bear so much he renamed his own teddy bear from Edward Bear to Winnie-the-Pooh. That's why the boy's father, A.A. Milne, used the name Winnie-the-Pooh in the stories that later became world famous.

As for a lion in Canadian military headquarters? Major McNaughton *did* keep a lion as a mascot. He rescued the cub from a zoo in Paris that was being shut down. The lion was not housebroken and spent most of its time with McNaughton in his office. McNaughton also sat beside the lion in his car as he toured back roads, much to the amazement of soldiers they passed.

THE IMPORTANCE OF VIMY RIDGE

The seven-kilometre (4.3 mi.) long Vimy Ridge in northern France, near Arras, held a commanding view over the surrounding countryside. Previous unsuccessful French and British attacks had suffered over 150,000 casualties.

In early 1917, British High Command ordered the Canadian Corps to capture the position as part of a larger spring offensive in the Arras area. In the coming campaign, British forces to the south would have limited success, and the French would fail badly, with many of their units reduced to mutiny. The Canadian attack against Vimy Ridge would be spectacular by comparison. . . .

The battle has since become an important symbol for Canada, the place where Canadians from across the country delivered an unprecedented victory, all four divisions of the Canadian Corps fighting together for the first time in the war.

—War Museum of Canada

GENERAL BYNG AND GENERAL MCNAUGHTON— NO CLASS DIVISIONS IN THE ARMY

In Britain, unlike the raw young country of Canada, class divisions in society were clearly marked and not to be crossed. The British army was the same: birth, marriage and social position played a big part in which officers were chosen to lead enlisted men. It was an elitism that did not always result in smart, capable officers. Men from the lower classes were expected to obey orders without question, no matter how bad an officer's decision might seem.

For the Canadians, however, class divisions were seen as undemocratic, and when a newly promoted Sergeant Cassels

was informed that he could not walk down the streets with a soldier who was a private, he tore off his stripes and declared that he was not a sergeant anymore.

Canadian officers reached their ranks based on their intelligence and leadership qualities. And Canadian soldiers were expected to think for themselves. General Byng made this statement to his Vimy sector in 1917: "What I want is the discipline of a well-trained pack of hounds. You find your own holes through the hedges. I'm not going to tell you where they are. But never lose sight of your objective. Reach it in your own way."

To help his officers and soldiers achieve this goal, Byng was very careful to give them the training to succeed, as shown in the next chapters.

Jake had not known that Lieutenant Norman could ride a horse, yet the officer was mounted on Coal Dust ahead, holding a pole with a red flag highly visible to the whole platoon.

It was a cold morning, with frost tingeing the chewed-up ground. Marching beside Charlie, Jake held his rifle at the position called high port, with the bayonet in place. This position would allow him to either lunge and use the rifle like a spear or drop the barrel and shoot.

"No lines!" Lieutenant Norman shouted at the men. "No lines! Clumps!"

A battle called the Somme Offensive had gone horribly for the Allies. Part of the reason was that, fighting traditionally, brigade after brigade had advanced in neat waves that made the soldiers easy targets for modern weaponry. General Byng had decided he didn't care about military tradition. If it didn't make sense to attack in lines, Canadian soldiers would do it differently.

A few other platoon soldiers moved ahead of Jake and Charlie to make the group more of a circle than a line. As they advanced, Jake continued counting his steps. He reached ninety. He expected the next order shortly and it came.

"Halt!" Lieutenant Norman shouted a few seconds later. "Check your watches."

"Welcome to the Vimy Glide," Charlie said to Jake. "How did we do?"

One step every few seconds. Precisely one hundred yards in three minutes. That was called the Vimy Glide. Each soldier needed to be able to move at that exact pace. One hundred yards in three minutes.

"Answer for yourself," Jake said. "That's the whole point of this."

At the brutal Battle of the Somme, too many officers had been taken out of action, and too few of the soldiers under their command knew enough to lead the others. General Byng had ensured that the Canadians would differ from the British and French troops in another way. The French and British did not believe their soldiers needed to be trained in tactics or battle strategy. But every Canadian, from junior officer down to the lowest ranked soldier, had been given a detailed responsibility and understood their role in the larger plan.

"I only think for myself when necessary," Charlie said. "I don't like to waste my energy when I can get others to do my work. So keep it up and I'll match you step for step."

Before Jake could answer, Lieutenant Norman gave another expected order. "Advance!"

The platoon was less than twenty-five paces from the enemy trench, marked by coils of barbed wire that protected the front lip. Lieutenant Norman spun his horse away to give the platoon a clear shot at the target.

Even this close, Jake and Charlie held back from charging. According to the plan, their pace had to be exact. No faster. No slower.

The sky was clouded and their bodies threw no shadows as they marched in a slow rhythm to the pace of the Vimy Glide.

Fifteen steps away. Then ten. Then five.

Finally, the moment to attack.

Jake shifted his rifle to his right hand. With his other hand, he reached into a pouch on his belt and grabbed a grenade.

The lead soldiers threw mats over the barbed wire. Jake and Charlie joined the platoon in a final rush over the mats to jump down into the enemy trench.

Jake landed on his feet and twisted sideways, alert for any attacking soldier.

He stared directly into the face of a defender. Jake reacted instantly. He tossed the grenade farther down the trench where it would do the most damage, far enough away that the explosion wouldn't hurt him or the other Canadians.

Then Jake lifted his rifle and pointed it at the defender.

"Surrender or die," Jake snarled. Jake shoved his rifle forward, stopping the bayonet only inches from the other soldier's chest.

"You may think you sound frightening," the enemy said. "But all I see is a farm boy who would like to go home. Not only that, but a farm boy who is still terrible at chess."

"Surrender or die," Jake snarled again.

"Is it only one or the other?" the enemy asked. "Can we not discuss another possibility?"

"Like what?" Jake said, lowering his rifle.

"I have become quite fond of tea," the enemy said. "Would it not be nice to sit down and share a pot and some conversation? I have no interest in surrendering or dying. Tea with two milk and two sugar and some chocolate would be much better."

"Sure, Thomas," Jake said. "You've got some chocolate left from the last mail call, right? Why *do* you get so many packages?"

Lieutenant Norman blew a whistle. Jake glanced upward from the trench bottom to see Lieutenant Norman's outline against the sky.

"Good work, men," Lieutenant Norman said. "Now we'll switch. Attackers become defenders. And defenders become attackers. One more time and then we'll break for lunch."

"See you in about fifteen minutes," Jake told Thomas. "Don't forget to pick up my dummy grenade as you go. It rolled into the corner behind you."

—·—

"I have never liked mules," Thomas said over his shoulder to Jake. "And yet, when our army has ten thousand to do the work, here I am, doing an excellent imitation of one."

The two of them walked one in front of the other in a trench. There was a light drizzle, and the mud at the bottom was slippery.

"It's Charlie's job to complain," Jake said. "Not yours. And he would be telling us that he'd get a servant to carry his load."

Jake and Thomas shared a sling filled with boxes of ammunition. Each end of the sling was attached to the center of each of their rifles.

"Charlie is right behind you," Charlie said. He, too, was carrying ammunition down the trench with another member of the platoon. Hundreds of pairs of soldiers formed a line. Their job was to carry the ammunition from wagons at the back of the line, through all of the trenches until they reached the defending posts at the edge of No Man's Land. All of this was to prepare for the attack on Vimy Ridge. "Charlie does not like it when you talk about Charlie."

"Does my friend Jake speak the truth?" Thomas asked.

"Would you not want all of us to know that in your mansion in Toronto you have a servant to do this kind of work for you?"

"Since you already know this, why bother explaining?" Charlie asked. "Besides, I'm beginning to believe that Toronto doesn't exist, that it was all a dream. So don't remind me of it, okay?"

"Watch out, Charlie," Jake said. "Once you lower yourself to our kind of life, we might actually start liking you."

"The horrors of war," Charlie said. "Anything but that."

Then Charlie laughed.

"I am beginning to like that man," Thomas said. "Perhaps I too am losing my mind. I am still impressed that he named my dog Colonel Scruffington. Who knew that Charlie had a sense of humor?"

"Again," Charlie said, "Charlie is right behind you and Charlie can hear every word. Move faster, please. And shut up. I have no intention of liking either of you in return."

It was impossible to move faster. The mud was too slippery, and it was awkward to keep balanced with the sling full of ammunition between Jake and Thomas.

"Don't let him hurt your feelings," Jake told Thomas. "He is still mad about losing to you in chess."

"He should not be angry," Thomas said. "Everyone loses to me in chess."

"If you are so smart," Charlie called ahead, "why are you packing ammo like an ordinary mule?"

Thomas was quiet, but only for a moment. Then he said, "Charlie, that is an excellent question. By tomorrow, I will have an answer for you."

—•—

"I have never liked mules," Thomas said to Jake. "You have heard me say this before, have you not?"

Thomas held the halter of a mule. He pulled, but the mule refused to move.

"At least it's not raining," Jake said. "And we're finally out of the trenches."

Now the platoon was on a large, gently sloping hill in an area miles away from the trenches at the base of Vimy Ridge. Most of the preparation work in the trenches was finished. Thousands and thousands of pounds of equipment and ammunition had already been moved to the front line by thousands and thousands of soldiers.

The platoon was scattered across the slope. This far from the front line, there was no danger.

"But we are out of the trenches with a *mule*," Thomas said. "This mule in particular. I think I will name him Charlie. Yes. Charlie the Mule."

Charlie the Mule was a sorrel—copper red—and his large ears were gray.

Thomas pulled at the halter again.

"How about pushing it," Jake said.

"Mules can kick in any direction," Thomas said. "And they are smart. Very smart. I prefer to stand here where his feet cannot reach me and where I can let him see that I mean business."

Thomas spoke directly to the mule. "Charlie, do not make me show you the wrath of a Cree warrior."

The pack on the mule was loaded with boxes filled with blue pennants. Charlie the Mule twitched his large ears and pulled his lips back, almost as if he was making a face at Thomas.

"Tell Charlie the Mule what you told McNaughton's lion," Jake said to Thomas. "That he will taste good after a little time on a stick over a campfire. Maybe he understands Cree."

"Mules understand everything," Thomas said. "But they are like cats. They just do not care. With cats, at least, you can pick them up and put them down where you tell them to go. This is not so with mules."

Thomas pulled on the halter and the mule remained as immovable as a wall.

"This is what I am talking about," Thomas said. "Charlie the Mule pretends I am not even here. Perhaps that means we should rest."

"Good idea," Jake said.

Jake and Thomas surveyed the hillside. The flags that the mule packed were there to add to the miles and miles of flags already fluttering in the cold breeze.

The platoon, along with dozens of other platoons, had nearly completed turning the vast hillside into a full-scale duplicate of the enemy's defense system on Vimy Ridge.

Colored tapes were strung for miles across the vast hill. Based on photography from air balloons and from reports of enemy soldiers captured during trench raids, these tapes marked every twist and turn of the enemy's known trenches.

Highly visible billboards were marked with the names of the German trenches. Pennants of different colors—like the pennants in the boxes that the mule packed—had been placed exactly where the enemy positions were at Vimy Ridge. Red pennants marked trenches. Yellow pennants marked machine guns. Blue pennants marked roads. Black pennants marked dugouts.

It didn't stop there.

Every clump of rolled barbed wire known to the Canadians had been marked. So had every suspected mine position.

Nothing like a training mission of this scope had ever been done before. But the stakes were high, and General Byng was not going to send his soldiers into battle without giving every man the best chance possible to accomplish the mission.

In a few days, when all was completed, the full training would begin, matching the smaller scale training when the platoon had had to learn the Vimy Glide. After full training here, the final battle at Vimy Ridge would involve the entire Canadian force. All four divisions. There had been no greater battle before in Canada's young history.

Jake knew all this. All of the soldiers knew this. It would be an epic battle.

Yes, Jake thought, an epic battle.

He grinned at a new thought.

Beside him was another epic battle.

Charlie the Mule against Thomas Northstar.

It would be very interesting to see which of the two was going to be more stubborn.

—·—

Charlie the Mule felt the pull on his halter. Charlie didn't mind following orders if the orders were put to him respectfully. If one of the two-legged creatures mistreated him, that was a different matter entirely. He never forgot abuse and would wait for a chance to return that abuse with a well-placed and unexcited kick.

But even if the two-legged creature treated him nicely, Charlie wasn't going to follow an order that might harm him. Sometimes, these smaller creatures had no sense of what was in front of them, but Charlie always knew.

Since he was far stronger than the two-legged creature trying to pull him forward, Charlie remained in place, flicking his tail calmly.

Sooner or later, the two-legged creature in front of him would learn why Charlie wasn't about to take another step.

Until then, Charlie had the time and the patience to wait until the silliness of the two-legged creature was finished.

—•—

"Charlie," Thomas told the mule, "I will stand here all day. Surely you are getting tired of this."

Thomas dug in his heels and pulled the halter as hard as he could.

"I don't think it is making *him* tired," Jake told Thomas. "But I know it's making me tired to watch you. Hand me the halter."

Thomas glared at Jake. "I will not let myself be defeated by a mule. It is as simple as that. Even if it means standing here for the remainder of the war."

"Please let me try," Jake said. "Remember, I grew up on a farm."

"Only if this is not seen as surrender."

"Of course not." Jake took the halter. He didn't try to move the mule forward. Instead, he turned it sideways and Charlie the Mule took a step in Jake's direction.

"Please give me that rope," Thomas said.

"See," Jake answered. "All you needed to do was choose a different direction."

"That means a longer path," Thomas said. "It also means that Charlie the Mule defeated Thomas the Cree. I will not accept that. This mule will go where I want it to go."

Thomas used the halter to turn Charlie the Mule back to the original path. Charlie the Mule braced his front legs and began to bray.

When the loud, hideous sound stopped, Jake said, "I think that means Charlie the Mule will not accept defeat either."

"Then we will be here until the war ends."

"Much as I enjoy seeing you finally lose at something," Jake said, "the platoon needs these pennants at the top of the hill. Before the war ends. So that we can end the war."

"Can you hand me that rock?" Thomas asked Jake, pointing at one about the size of a softball. "Charlie the Mule needs to learn a lesson."

"No!" Jake said. "Thomas. It's not right to hit him with a rock. And you'll feel bad about it later. I won't let you do that to Charlie. Or to yourself."

"Hit the mule?" Thomas said, still holding the halter. "That is not my intent. Anyone who even kicks an animal is a weakling. Now would you please give me that rock."

Jake handed it over to Thomas.

"You must listen to me," Thomas said to Charlie the Mule. "While I would never use a rock on a stubborn mule, someday your stubbornness might anger another soldier who would."

Thomas touched the rock to the mule's nose. "Imagine how much that would hurt if someone hit you with this."

The donkey brayed.

"He's laughing at you," Jake said. "Obviously he doesn't know you are like a North Star to guide us whenever times are dark."

"He's laughing because he knows I told you I would never hurt him. Maybe I should shoot a couple bullets to scare him."

"It would scare everyone else too," Jake said. "Not a good idea."

"Then I will think of something else," Thomas said. He was facing the mule as he spoke.

"I know," Thomas said. "I will pretend he likes to chase things like Colonel Scruffington."

Thomas said to the mule, "Fetch."

He heaved the large rock over his shoulder in the direction he wanted the mule to go.

When the rock landed, a tremendous boom knocked Jake onto his back.

He stared at the sky, trying to figure out what had just happened. Clods of dirt rained onto his face.

He rolled over and saw Charlie the Mule on his side. Thomas had landed on Charlie. Thomas had a stunned and dazed look on his face.

Jake looked past Thomas at a hole deep enough to bury Charlie the Mule.

That's when he realized what had happened.

There had been an unexploded artillery shell in the ground. This was very common, even far away from the front line of trench warfare. It wasn't unusual for soldiers, or even farmers, to step on one of the shells or bump one of the shells and cause a deadly explosion.

Charlie the Mule had saved their lives.

Charlie the Mule did a half roll and got to his feet. Thomas got up too and hung onto Charlie's side to keep his balance. His eyes were wide and he tried to speak but couldn't say a word.

"Hey, Thomas," Jake said. He wiped dirt from his face. "You sure taught that mule a lesson, didn't you."

—•—

Joseph Wright, the man across the chessboard from Jake, was a soldier from a nearby platoon. They were halfway through the game, at the far end of a large tent that had been set up to feed soldiers.

Thomas sat nearby, watching the game. Colonel Scruffington sat at his feet, tongue hanging out.

Jake moved his queen and said, "Checkmate."

Joseph stood and saluted.

"Well, thanks," Jake said, "I thought it was a pretty good move, myself. Right, Thomas?"

No answer. Thomas was standing too, looking over Jake's shoulder. Colonel Scruffington had one paw on his eye, in a salute like Thomas had trained him.

Jake realized it must be a visiting officer if everyone was going to be this official. He scrambled to his feet.

Major McNaughton was walking toward them.

"At ease, soldiers," Major McNaughton said. "We're all in the same army."

Thomas had trained Colonel Scruffington to put his paw down when he heard the phrase "at ease."

Major McNaughton smiled at that. "Aahh, yes. Our British colonel."

Major McNaughton looked at Jake and Thomas. "Good to see you again. I heard a story that Charlie helped you find an unexploded shell out on the training grounds. Excellent work. No doubt you saved the lives of at least a couple of soldiers."

"We will pass that on to Charlie," Jake said.

"I just spoke to him," Major McNaughton said. "Strange thing is, he pretended not to know what I was talking about. He insisted I didn't need to thank him."

"Yes, sir," Thomas said. "Charlie is very stubborn. A real mule."

"Very stubborn," Jake added. "Definitely a mule."

"Sometimes, stubborn is not a bad thing," Major McNaughton said. "Anyway, Thomas, I want to talk to you about how you broke the rules in the trenches. A complaint reached Lieutenant

Norman that you and Jake did not ask permission from nearby officers to stop carrying ammunition in a sling."

Thomas kept his shoulders square and his head high. "Lieutenant Norman was at the other end of the trenches, so I tried to show one officer that there was a better way to do it. He refused to listen. I thought that the only way to prove that it worked would be to do it."

Anger crossed Major McNaughton's face.

"I don't like this," Major McNaughton said, "but before I make a judgment, tell me exactly what you did."

"It is called a tumpline," Thomas said. "A broad strap across the forehead, tied to the weight at the other end, and the weight hangs down your back. It keeps your hands free. It helps you keep your balance and you can move faster. Fur traders and Cree use them to carry heavy loads through the forest. It seemed a better way to move through the trenches."

Jake said. "It is my fault, Major McNaughton. Thomas made it look so easy that I tried it. I was the one who said we should go ahead even if that officer didn't want to listen. Punish me, not Thomas."

"Punish you?" Major McNaughton said. "That is the last thing on my mind. Lieutenant Norman told me that you managed to move double the number of boxes of everyone else. I am going to have a chat with that officer and he will regret not listening to you. After that, we are going to get everyone else to start moving boxes the same way."

Major McNaughton turned his attention to the chessboard.

"It's been a while since I played this game, but I think I have the hang of it. Jake, would you like a game?"

"Major McNaughton," Jake said, "perhaps you should play Thomas and teach him a thing or two."

THE MULE WITH NO NAME

THE INSPIRATION BEHIND THE STORY OF

CHARLIE THE MULE

I believe that every soldier who has anything to do with horse or mule has come to love them for what they are and the grand work they have done and are doing in and out of the death zones.
—British officer Captain Sidney Galtrey, autumn 1918

Mules are a combination of horse and donkey. It is a wonderful combination, because they have the tremendous athletic  skill of a horse and the superior intelligence of a donkey. A horse's instinct is to take advantage of its speed and flee any kind of danger before giving thought to the

danger. Donkeys will sometimes decide that fighting is a
better solution, so donkeys
tend to try to decide what to do
before doing it. Because of that
donkey heritage, mules do not
frighten easily and are more
patient than a horse.

A horse caught in the barbed
wire of No Man's Land might
fight the wire in a panic and
get tangled far worse. A mule
would calmly try to understand the situation and wait for help.
A horse might carry a load until it died from exhaustion. Mules
know their limits and if forced to carry too much, simply would
not move.

Mules also have amazing smell and hearing, and can detect
trouble that humans will not. When a mule makes a decision
based on this information, it cannot be prodded to go into danger, unlike horses, who can be forced forward by riders. So
while it may seem that mules are stubborn, their hesitation is a
sign of intelligence.

Although the phrase "stubborn as a mule" is usually meant
as insult, it should probably be taken as a compliment.

Equally important during World War One was the fact that
mules do not need as much food as horses and are better able to
handle heat and cold. Better yet, they can last longer without
water, and during battles where clean water was scarce, this
made a big difference.

Mules also proved to be tougher than horses. They were
less affected by disease and died from infection from bullet
wounds half as often as horses. It is no surprise, then, that well

over a quarter million mules were used throughout the course of the war.

THE MULE WITH NO NAME

Among the soldiers who handled mules, it was widely understood that mules would not respond to any kind of punishment. Instead, it was said, that mules would remember who mistreated them and use that knowledge against the soldier in

the future.

These handlers also found that mules had a "sixth sense" when it came to danger. While it often frustrated the handlers and looked like plain old stubbornness, this awareness of surroundings and situations saved loads and lives.

One mule in particular was traveling down a soft steep hillside, and a portion of the hill began to slide loose. This mule had the presence of mind to buck his handler off his back to safety. As the hill continued to collapse, the mule also managed to free itself of a precious load of mail before the massive shift of dirt swept it away. All who saw this declared the mule deserved a medal.

THE NEAR IMPOSSIBILITY OF TAKING VIMY RIDGE

As part of a plan for the Allied forces to break through the German trench system, it was considered extremely important to take Vimy Ridge, and in 1917 this near-impossible task was given to the Canadians.

Vimy Ridge was 8 kilometers (5 mi.) long and up to 110 meters (360 ft.) high. The ridge dominated the landscape and had been captured early in the war by the Germans, who made it into a very strong defensive position, guarded by highly trained soldiers armed with devastating machine guns and artillery.

At the beginning of the war, some British officers thought the machine gun was an improper form of warfare, not to mention heavy and cumbersome, so the British Army essentially dismissed it as a weapon and entered the war with only a few hundred of them.

But as they showed with the first poison gas attacks, the Germans were not bound by traditional views on how gentlemen officers fought battles. They saw the potential in this single weapon that could provide as much firepower as hundreds of rifles. At the beginning of the war, they had 12,000 machine guns and eventually reached 100,000.

Machine guns tended to jam, so they were grouped together in fixed positions, often in concrete "pillboxes" along the trenches. A machine gun was set on a tripod, and it took a crew of 4 to 6 soldiers feeding the fabric belt of bullets to maintain a firing rate of 400 to 600 rounds per minute. (By the end of the war, this rate doubled, and machine guns also included one-man portable guns.)

So with up to five machine guns firing, a small group of men could spray the open land in front of them with up to 3,000 bullets per minute, a staggering 50 bullets per second. Because of this incredible rate of firing, the massed infantry attacks that had worked in earlier wars

were futile, but it was a lesson that the French and British high command often seemed to ignore. On the first day of the Battle of Somme, for example, the British suffered over 57,000 casualties—a total, in a matter of hours, that was greater than the combined British casualties of the Crimean, Boer and Korean wars.

Vimy Ridge, with its high vantage point and secure pillboxes that covered all the angles of attack, was so well defended that in 1914 and 1915, the French and British troops had suffered hundreds of thousands of casualties in trying to take Vimy Ridge from the Germans and had not succeeded.

When the Canadian soldiers attacked, they would be crossing an open graveyard, where the bodies of tens of thousands of fallen French and British soldiers still remained.

THE DUPLICATE VIMY RIDGE

"Chaps, you shall go over exactly like a railroad train, on time, or you shall be annihilated." This was the warning by General Julian Byng.

At the Battle of Somme, some entire brigades had been ordered to advance in neat waves, with no idea of the strategy of battle or even a specific location to reach. The Canadian high commanders had a response to this, as explained by General Arthur Currie, who said, "Take time to train them."

And as noted by Byng's warning, this training was designed to help the soldiers follow a plan as precise as a train timetable.

Behind the trenches, on broad slopes in the Vimy area, the Canadians undertook something on a scale that was unheard of before then—troops rehearsed the battle again and again. Miles and miles of tape and thousands of flags marked replicas of the actual German trenches. This included suspected mine positions, machine gun locations and barbed wire tangles. Again and again, troops practiced the Vimy Glide, with officers on horseback representing the advance shelling that would give them cover during the real attack. This ensured that soldiers covered exactly 100 yards (91 m) in exactly 180 seconds.

A second and important innovation was that the soldiers were trained to advance in small clumps, widely spread apart from other clumps. This was a significant change in tactics because it defied the military tradition of sending men forward in lines: lines that were far too easily shredded by machine gun fire.

CANADIAN INGENUITY ON THE FRONT

From the beginning of the war, the Germans had held an advantage in weapons, and their grenade launchers were no different, capable of sending grenades twice as far as British launchers.

Nicknamed Whizbang, Lieutenant-Colonel George Chalmers Johnston, the commander of the Second Canadian Mounted Rifles, wondered if shorter rifle barrels would give more thrust to escaping gases and decided to experiment.

By sawing nearly a foot off a rifle barrel to solve the problem, he technically committed a war crime: destroying government property. But he also discovered that the grenades went twice as far.

General Byng's response was to encourage this and other ingenuity. When Byng saw how much further the grenades went with the shorter rifles, he did not discipline Johnston but instead approved that all rifle grenade sections had sawed-off weapons.

It was no different with the tumpline. In an article in *Canadian Military History* magazine, F.R. Phelan describes how he helped save hundreds of man hours by introducing the tumpline, something he learned on camping trips in Quebec from watching First Nations men carry loads easily through the woods. Of equal importance is that one of his superior officers was open to trying this new method.

Lieutenant-Colonel Andrew McNaughton had a similarly open mind when it came to the new science of triangulation to identify the location of enemy artillery. This meant pinpointing the source of a sound by marking it from three locations. Traditional British gunners considered this to be "radical nonsense" and even laughed at the common sense suggestion that wind and weather might affect accuracy, but McNaughton encouraged the three scientists who believed in the idea, and they developed a system capable of locating a gun down to a range of a small circle and also taught gunners how wind and humidity affected the aiming points of artillery.

T his was not a drill. This was not practice. This was a real trench raid. At night.

The Storming Normans were one of the three platoons sent to cross the three hundred yards from their trenches to the enemy's trenches on the other side of No Man's Land.

No one would ever say there was a perfect night to attack. Not in war. It wasn't a game.

But conditions were as good as possible to reduce the danger.

There was no moon out, and the sky was clouded. There would be no light to betray the slow movements of the soldiers.

No sound either.

It had not rained in a week, and the shell-torn ground was soft but not sticky. The soldiers had fanned out to crawl across the ground in clumps of two or three. Each had been given a specific location to either throw mats on the barbed wire that guarded the enemy's trenches or crawl beneath it.

Jake knew part of the reason for tonight's trench raid was to take prisoners. Each new raid brought more prisoners, and those prisoners were valuable because they could share information.

For a successful attack on Vimy Ridge, General Byng and Major McNaughton needed to know as much as possible. Where were all the machine gun nests? How many enemy soldiers waited in which trenches? When were soldiers rotated from the front to the reserves?

Jake knew there was a new reason, however. And it had made every soldier in the platoon even more determined to succeed on this raid.

The day before, enemy prisoners had taunted the Canadians.

"Wait and see," they said. "The Prussians have joined us. They'll show you what real soldiers are like."

Because of that, rumors had flown up and down the trenches.

Prussians! Professional soldiers, with centuries of tradition. Their presence was a tremendous boost to the morale of the enemy.

So the Canadian platoons—formed by farmers and ranchers and accountants and bankers and schoolteachers and carpenters—had decided nobody was going to intimidate them.

Tonight was going to prove to the enemy that the ones to be feared were the Canadians.

—·—

On some evenings, the raiders had a simple job. They sneaked across No Man's Land and then crawled to the edge of the enemy trenches and spied on the activities. They would report back to the officers on what they had learned.

On other evenings, like this one, the raid would take them down into the enemy trenches. With all raids, the planning was precise. Not down to the minute. But down to the second.

Tonight—exactly forty-five minutes after leaving their own trenches—shelling would start to protect their retreat. Any soldier still in the enemy trenches would be in danger of being hit by those shells.

As he pushed himself along the ground on his elbows, Jake mentally rehearsed his own role in the raid. He was supposed to crawl under barbed wire at a location near the enemy's central machine gun nest, with Thomas and Charlie beside him. Once in position, they were to wait until Lieutenant Norman fired three quick shots. That would be the signal for the dozens and dozens of Canadian soldiers to rush into the enemy trenches. Jake, Charlie and Thomas each had sticks of dynamite to throw at the machine guns. They needed to time it perfectly so that those machine guns would not stop the other Canadian soldiers.

No Man's Land was like what Jake imagined the surface of the moon to be. The ground was barren, with deep craters. There was no sign of any vegetation, except remainders of trees long since blasted to small jagged stumps. The difference, he thought, was that the moon would have no water. Here, the deeper craters held stinking ponds of greenish slime.

He thought about the sticks of dynamite strapped on his back, in a place that would keep them dry from any mud as he crawled. He'd have to light the fuse, hold it until he knew the fuse would not sputter out, then throw it and duck his head as he waited for the explosion.

He gave it more thought, planning how he would—

An intense, bright red streak blossomed above him.

Flare!

Three more followed, lighting the dark sky.

Then star shells. These were fired straight up by the enemy, and once high enough, a white magnesium flare would burn from the shell. The shells would drift slowly down by parachute as the flare burned itself out, as dazzling as the sun.

Jake did not panic.

Nor did the soldiers around him.

Each simply froze in position. The slightest movement would betray a soldier's position. It would draw fire not only to that soldier, but to those around him.

When a soldier managed to fight the panic and not flinch or tremble, the soldier would simply become part of the cratered landscape, impossible to see among the tree stumps, no matter how bright the sky.

Jake had been caught in an awkward position. He had his left elbow on the ground and his right elbow raised. He had no choice but to hold that position until the red flares faded and the final white of the magnesium star shell had drifted onto the ground.

Safe.

He resumed his crawl forward, nearly blind. His eyes needed to adjust to the darkness again, but he couldn't stop. The time had been set for exactly when Lieutenant Norman would fire the shots to begin the raid and for when the raid would end.

No matter the price that Jake needed to pay, he would not fail his fellow soldiers. This was not bravery. It was dedication. He took comfort knowing that every other soldier in the platoon had the same determination.

—·—

As Jake, Charlie and Thomas reached the far side of No Man's Land, they split apart to jump into the enemy trench in different places. As Jake crawled beneath the first rolls of barbed wire, his uniform snagged at the shoulder.

Jake tried to inch backward, but another strand snagged his pants.

It was a horrible feeling, to be stuck. No way forward. No way back.

Worse, each second of delay was dangerous. Not only to him, but to the other soldiers of the platoon. If he was stuck, they'd have to come back to rescue him.

Jake told himself to be smart. He took a deep breath and did nothing. That was smart. It forced him not to panic.

He took another deep breath.

With his free arm, he reached down to his belt for a pair of wire clippers. He wanted to snip the wire right away. But he was so close to the enemy trench that the sound would carry and warn the soldiers in the trenches that an attack was about to happen.

He took another deep breath.

Wait, he told himself. Just wait.

Then it came. The three shots from Lieutenant Norman to send all of the Canadians into the enemy trenches.

Jake wished he could be there with his friends. But the best thing he could do was free himself so that he wouldn't put them in danger.

There was shouting and the sounds of explosions. No one would hear him clip the wire now. A minute later, he had freed himself.

He resumed crawling forward. When he reached the edge of the trench, he remained on his belly. He found the sticks of dynamite and lit the fuses. He tossed the sticks of dynamite toward the machine gun nest.

Seconds after the dynamite exploded, another flare went off. This was from behind Jake. At their own trenches. It was a signal for all the Canadians to scramble back from the raid.

Jake moved backward, hugging the ground.

Other soldiers swarmed up and over the trenches, running in a crouch toward the Canadian side.

Halfway across No Man's Land, above the *crack-crack-crack* of rifle shots, came a shout. "Jake!"

It was Thomas.

"Thomas!" Jake shouted.

"Help!" Thomas said. "I've been hit."

Jake didn't hesitate. He stopped and turned in the dark. He couldn't see his friend.

In the night, in the quiet, it was foolish to betray your location with any noise. But now, with rifles firing, it didn't matter.

"Where?" Jake shouted.

"Here!"

Jake crawled toward the sound. It didn't take him long to find his friend.

"Not good," Thomas said. "My leg. I can't move."

"I'll drag you," Jake said.

"No," Thomas said above the shots coming from the enemy trench. "Then they might hit you too. Help me find a way to stop the bleeding, then run and save yourself."

Jake was about to say something, but then it felt like his leg had been hit by a baseball bat.

He toppled. As he landed, he realized that he had also been shot.

—•—

In twos and threes, the soldiers of the Storming Normans dropped safely back into their trench on the other side of No Man's Land.

As Charlie looked up and down the trench, he felt the satisfaction of accomplishing a difficult task.

He also felt the satisfaction of belonging to a team. He'd never had that kind of satisfaction before, and he knew why. Before the war, he had depended on his family name and his family money to get respect. Now he realized it was a hollow respect.

Lance Wesley had been right all those months ago. Here was

a place where a person was judged only on his merits. Charlie had earned respect, and it felt great. It also felt great to be Canadian, among the soldiers who were revered up and down the trenches among the British and French because of their boldness and toughness.

Yes, sir, Charlie thought, with rumors flying that the Prussians would show the Canadians a thing or two about fighting, just the opposite had happened.

The light from lanterns showed that at least six of the Prussians had been captured from the enemy trenches.

This would show who ruled No Man's Land!

The captured Prussians would have valuable information for the Canadian commanders. Every new bit of knowledge made it that much easier for the Canadians when they attacked Vimy Ridge.

Every soldier knew it would happen. Every soldier knew how it would happen. That had been the purpose of months of training.

But only the high commanders knew *when* it would happen. That was too important to risk leaking to the enemy.

Along with pride and satisfaction, Charlie felt triumph. While he was reluctant to admit to Jake and Thomas how much he liked them, he wanted to be with them to share the triumph.

Except, as he walked up and down the trenches, he couldn't find them. He only found Colonel Scruffington, who gave an anxious whine.

His stomach began to fill with dread.

Charlie made his way to Lieutenant Norman, followed by Colonel Scruffington.

"Jake and Thomas," Charlie said to Lieutenant Norman. "Have you seen them?"

Lieutenant Norman shook his head. "I've been searching for them too. Everyone is back except for them."

"Let me volunteer," Charlie said. "I want to go back out there and look for them."

"Not tonight," Lieutenant Norman said. "It's too dangerous. The enemy is smarting from what we just did and they will want to get revenge by stopping any rescue attempts out there. With lights to help you search, they'll shoot you in seconds. Without lights, you will be wandering like a blind person with no chance of finding them."

"Then, with all respect," Charlie said, "I'll sneak out and look for them without your permission. Little chance of finding them is better than no chance staying here in the trenches."

"I appreciate your loyalty to your fellow soldiers," Lieutenant Norman said. "But tonight, we have help from the French. They've sent out their mercy dogs. If Jake and Thomas are alive, those dogs will find them long before you could. So stay with me, and let's trust in those animals."

—·—

Biscotte was a Belgian shepherd. She was a medium-sized dog, with perky ears and silky black fur.

She leaped over the top of the trench and began a zigzag pattern across the open ground. She wore small saddlebags of canvas. These contained bandages and other first aid remedies.

Biscotte did not flinch as the occasional bullet whizzed over her head. She froze when a flare lit the sky.

Then the slightest of breezes brought her the scent of human blood. She was accustomed to the smell. But there was a difference in the scent between a wounded soldier and one that was beyond all help.

Biscotte drew another breath through her nostrils.

Alive!

This blood came from a human that needed her.

Biscotte leaped forward, sure-footed on the treacherous ground. Her vision showed the outlines of stumps and the deep craters. She avoided all the dangers and pushed forward.

Nearer and nearer. The scent grew stronger and filled her with excitement that made her quiver.

She did not bark. That was part of her training. A barking noise would draw enemy attention, and with it the bullets of snipers.

Instead, Biscotte swallowed a whimper of that excitement and pushed forward.

As the scent of the blood grew stronger, she realized it was not one human soldier. But two.

And both were alive!

—•—

"Don't worry," Jake told Thomas. "I don't think anyone has died from a bullet through the butt cheeks."

Maybe later, if they had a chance to tell their stories, it would be funny. But stuck in No Man's Land, with Thomas barely able to crawl, there was nothing funny about the situation.

"Not bullet," Thomas said. "Bullets. You told me you counted two. And it feels like twenty."

Jake had tied his belt tight on his thigh to slow the bleeding from a bullet that had torn through muscle just above his knee. There wasn't much he could do for Thomas without some bandages. Or for himself.

"One bullet. Two," Jake said, trying to be cheerful. "Not much difference once you've been hit."

Jake had tried to stand on his wounded leg. He had toppled over after trying one step.

"It's not the bullets that worry me," Thomas said. "It is the infection."

Jake was silent at that. More often than not, a bullet drove small pieces of uniform into the wound, and the dirtiness of the fabric was what started the infection.

What they both needed, as much as any kind of help, was disinfectant to pour into their wounds. That would help in the crucial few hours right after being shot.

Jake was silent thinking about that too. The darkness protected the two of them from being seen by the enemy. But it also prevented a nighttime search by any of the Storming Normans. Candle flames and flashlights would draw gunfire from the enemy.

"You need to go," Thomas said. "At least you can crawl."

"If enemy soldiers find us, I'll be here to fight with you," Jake said. "So shut up about me leaving you, okay? We'll tell each other stories to pass time. I want to know if you ever played one of the priests at your school in chess."

Thomas didn't reply at first. Then Thomas said, "Some stories are best not told. And some stories are hard to understand if you did not grow up where I did."

Jake heard a lot of pain in that statement. Not shot-with-a-bullet pain. But long-carried pain.

"Thomas," he said, "by now, you and I are brothers. Even if we don't make it through the night, I want you to know that."

Thomas again did not reply. Distant shots and distant shouts broke the silence.

Then Thomas spoke in a quiet voice. "The only reason I studied chess was because someday, if I had the chance, I wanted to beat them at their game. The priests treated us like animals, and I wanted to show them we are not."

"And?"

"I beat all three of them. Then all three of them beat me."

"I don't understand," Jake said.

"One by one, I put each of them into checkmate. So I beat them, just as I had dreamed."

"Then you played again and they won?"

"No. They refused to play me again. But they beat me. They told me I needed to learn my place. So they used sticks and beat me."

Jake felt his fury grow. It made him forget about the deep throbbing pain in his thigh. "When this is over, let me go back there with you."

"What would it prove?" Thomas asked. "That someone like me needs a white person to protect me? That I can't protect myself?"

Jake said, "I would not be going there as a white person. I would be going as your friend."

"They would not see it that way," Thomas said. "It is not just the priests at the school, you know. The land agents and bankers are against us too. That's why I need citizenship. As a citizen, I would be equal to those who do not let my people farm and raise cattle like any other farmer and rancher in the country. I have one medal already, and if I can, I will fight to get as many more as possible. Then how can anyone in my country deny me citizenship?"

Before Jake could answer, it seemed like a piece of black detached itself from the night beside him. Not until he felt a tongue lick his cheek did he realize it was a dog.

—•—

Charlie paced the trenches. He was still tempted to risk punishment and crawl back into No Man's Land. If Jake and Thomas were still alive, they needed help. If they were still alive, they needed to be rescued before daylight, when the enemy would see them out in the open.

If—

He heard a shout in French.

"Viens ici!"

Charlie knew just enough French to understand that someone had yelled, "Come here!"

With Colonel Scruffington behind him, Charlie hurried down the trench, cursing each new glob of mud that clung to his boots and slowed his progress. But maybe he wasn't about to get good news. Maybe he should just stay where he was and let the mud prevent him from learning something that he dreaded hearing.

Lieutenant Norman was already there.

The lanterns showed the French handler was patting the head of a medium-sized dog, black and silky.

The dog's saddlebag was open.

Charlie instantly understood what that meant. Someone—out there in No Man's Land—had been able to take out the first aid supplies. That meant someone—out there in No Man's Land—was alive.

"Bien, Biscotte," the French soldier said. He patted the dog's head. *"Bien"*

The French soldier pulled two pieces of cloth out of the dog's mouth. He held the pieces of uniform out for Lieutenant Norman.

It didn't matter to Charlie that he couldn't understand the rest of what the French soldier said. Charlie knew that the mercy dogs would tear a piece of uniform from a wounded soldier and bring it back to the handler. Then the dog would lead men back out to the injured.

Two pieces. Two soldiers.

The flickering light showed that the pieces came from uniforms that belonged to Canadian soldiers.

"Hold it to the Colonel," Charlie said. "Let him have a sniff."

Lieutenant Norman knelt to the dog. Colonel Scruffington caught the scent and began to prance and whine. He'd been taught not to bark in the trenches.

"Sir," Charlie said immediately to Lieutenant Norman, "I'll go. I'll follow the dog back out to them. We won't need lights, so the enemy won't be able to see us. We will be safe."

Lieutenant Norman hesitated, but only a fraction of a second. "Find some stretchers," Lieutenant Norman said. "We'll take two other men, and the four us should have them back in the trenches in no time at all."

PRUSCO AND MICHAEL

THE INSPIRATION BEHIND THE STORY OF
BISCOTTE

Prusco was a French dog that looked like a white wolf. Like all mercy dogs, Prusco had been trained to find wounded soldiers and not to bark when he found one, as this would draw gunfire from the enemy.

During one battle, Prusco allowed an injured soldier to hold onto his collar and dragged the soldier into a depression, safe from enemy fire. He repeated this to save the lives of three soldiers that day. In all, Prusco is credited with saving more than a hundred lives.

A French Red Cross dog named Michael, as trained, returned from the battlefield with the glove of a wounded soldier named Henri. Michael led first aid attendants to a remote part of the

battlefield where Henri was lying. The doctor examined Henri and declared him dead.

Again and again, Michael returned to the medics to try to make them come back to Henri. They ignored him, and eventually Michael disappeared until late that night, when a French guard noticed an eerie sight—a large dark object moving closer and closer: Michael, returning with Henri, dragging the man along the ground.

That's when medics took another look and realized Henri was breathing. They rushed him to the hospital where he recovered from his battlefield wounds.

LUXURY IN ENEMY TRENCHES

Because the Germans were first to choose their defensive positions, they occupied the high ground, which meant that rainwater traveled down from their trenches to form the miserable mud endured by the Allies. The Germans also had the time to create huge dugouts to serve as meeting rooms, kitchens and full-sized living quarters.

The luxury was impressive enough to make it into a 1916 issue of *Architectural Digest*, where an Allied officer described a captured German trench that was "designed to house a whole company of 300 men, with the needful kitchens, provisions and munitions storerooms . . . an engine room and a motor room; many of the captured dugouts were thus lighted by electricity . . . [In] the officers' quarters, there have been found full-length mirrors, comfortable bedsteads, cushioned armchairs, and some pictures."

Another Allied soldier described finding in the German trenches "a veritable home from home, with bread and bottles of wine on tables. There was also a piano, the top of which was covered with picture postcards."

In contrast, the British and Canadian officers saw their own rough trenches as something that would not allow their soldiers to become soft.

Maybe it was this toughness that made the difference when it came to trench raids in the dark: Germans soldiers rarely ventured away from their trenches, while Canadian soldiers grew bolder and bolder in attacks on the Germans at night.

THE TRENCH RAID

At night, small teams of Canadian soldiers would use burned cork to make their faces black, then cross No Man's Land and drop into the enemy trenches. Their mission was to capture enemy soldiers, disable machine guns, gather intelligence material such as maps and written orders, and demoralize the enemy.

Trench raids were a Canadian invention. Nobody else on either side had considering raiding the enemy during the stretches of time between major battles. The Princess Pats, as the Princess Patricia's Canadian Light Infantry was known, decided to try it in February 1915, by sending one hundred men across in a "smash-and-grab" attack. In November of the same year, the 7th Battalion (British Columbia) took this one step further. The front had been quiet and the Canadian soldiers were bored, so 170 volunteers rehearsed an attack for ten days, and when they struck, only two of the soldiers were hurt in a raid that was so successful that it became a model for future raids. As a result, the Canadians became the acknowledged experts on trench raids.

And in January of 1917, Calgary soldiers from the 50th Battalion learned from a prisoner captured during a raid that the Prussians—trained professionals with a long military tradition—were about to enter the line. The prisoner warned the Canadians—who came from varied backgrounds like teaching, accounting and farming—that the Prussians would show them what "real" soldiers were like.

In response, the 50th organized another raid as the Prussians were moving into place and still not organized, and they captured Prussian prisoners to deliver back to the Canadian trenches.

"Please do not take this as a complaint," Thomas said to Jake. "But I do not like this at all."

"Because you have to stop singing to complain," Jake said, "I'd be happy if you kept complaining. Also, you are so off tune, I think it is cruel to make the horses listen to you."

Each of them were holding the reins of a packhorse. The horses carried canvas bags, one bag on each side. Each bag held four massive shells that looked like gigantic bullets. Two shells together weighed as much as a full-grown man.

Just beyond them were the massive guns that fired those shells. It took a team of twenty men to load those guns. And there were nearly a thousand artillery pieces firing at the enemy.

Jake and Thomas were in a group of hundreds of soldiers who had been given the job of leading the packhorses from the rail lines to the guns.

Jake shifted his feet. He was standing in muddy water. His leg was sore from where the bullet had torn through his thigh six weeks earlier. He was covered in slime from mud. He itched from lice. His hands were cold.

"Besides," Jake said, "it is just another day in paradise. Why would any of us complain?"

"I just said it was not a complaint. I said—"

Thomas did not get to finish his sentence. A new barrage of shells thundered. It had been like this for seven full days.

Thousands of shells each day and night rained down on the enemy trenches. Thousands!

Soon, the Canadians would advance. But until then, the enemy would not be given time to eat or sleep or even time to shave. They would be getting tired from constantly being ready for battle.

In the short silence that followed, Thomas finished speaking. "What I do not like is how horrible it is for these horses. You and I had a choice. We volunteered. And we can speak when we need help. Not these horses."

Thomas pointed at his horse. "Louise here, she—"

"Louise?"

"She reminds me of my aunt Louise. Very patient. We can pick off the lice from our skin, but these sores? Mange. From mites. She must be in constant pain, but she does not fight her load or kick at me."

Thomas ran his hand along her ribs. "Have you noticed each day we have to cinch the straps another hole? These horses are starving."

Thomas lifted Louise's front foot. "This hoof. It is like all the others on Louise. You are a farm boy. You know what that is. This horse is miserable."

The hoof was splitting because it was constantly wet. Jake sighed. "Canker."

Thomas knocked on his helmet. "I have protection. This horse does not. Horses are shot at and shelled and hit with poison gas. When this war is over, I hope they are given good treatment. They deserve it."

Before Jake could reply, another huge round of shells thundered from the big guns. It was too loud to hear conversation, even if someone had shouted in his ear.

As it turned out, someone *was* trying to shout in his ear.

Jake felt a hand on his shoulder and turned.

Charlie's face was filthy with mud, but he had a wide, white grin.

As the thunder lessened, Charlie said. "Hey you two! Lieutenant Norman sent me to look for you. The doctors cleared you to join the platoon for active service. We all cheered when we heard. You can come back with me straight away."

"No," Thomas said.

"No?" Charlie echoed. "In the hospital, you said you would do anything to get back to the fight."

"That has not changed," Thomas said. "But these two horses depend on Jake and me to get them back for the night. Then we will join the platoon."

—•—

"This is like mail call for Thomas," Lance Wesley told Jake. "Chocolates for him. Wagonloads of feed for the horses. Even some barrels with oats."

They stood in a field, surrounded by hundreds of other packhorses and hundreds of other soldiers.

There was only a half hour of sunlight left. Wind was picking up with the first traces of sleet. None of them commented on the weather. In Canada, they had faced much worse without complaint. They took pride in this, knowing the British and French soldiers marveled at a Canadian soldier's toughness and endurance.

Lance's hearing had returned, but he had an obvious limp that kept him from active duty, so he had not been cleared for battle.

Lance ran his hand along Louise's right front leg, feeling for injuries. He cared very much about all the horses.

He frowned. "Anywhere else and any other time, these horses would be getting rest and feed. I am glad, Thomas, that you donate all your chocolate and treats for the horses, but they need more than that."

"I am very aware of this," Thomas said. "I wish I could do more."

Lance said to Thomas, "What's your secret? Why do you get so many packages with chocolate from so many women?"

"There is no secret," Thomas said. "It should be obvious. A fine warrior like me turns heads anywhere."

"Either that," Jake said, "or a fine warrior like him is very good at writing letters."

"Letters?" Lance asked.

"Letters?" Thomas said, trying to sound innocent.

"Thomas," Jake said, "I found one of your half-written letters where you had dropped it. I put it back in your notebook while you were asleep. Of course, I read it first. Such sweet words to a lady in London named Nancy. And of course, I then looked for other letters in your notebook. And found other names."

"Oh," Thomas said. "*Those* letters. I only do it because it makes all of them so happy to help a poor, lonely soldier. It is a sacrifice, but someone must do it."

Lance said, "I don't understand."

"British newspapers," Jake said. "There's a column called 'Lonely Soldier.' It's for soldiers at the front without friends or relatives who write to the newspapers and give their names. Women in England send food and candy and letters to cheer up the lonely soldiers."

Thomas grinned at Lance and Jake. "It was one of your people who said that the pen is mightier than the sword. I am happy to learn your ways when it is convenient or useful. After all, that is why I use army socks in Cree moccasins."

Lance laughed. "I'm going to miss you, both of you. It's been nice to have a couple of weeks with mates from the platoon. But I understand why you want to get back."

Soldiers in a platoon were closer than brothers. They fought hard in battle because they did not want to let down their brothers in arms.

Jake knew that Thomas had an extra motivation, however. Thomas believed if he returned to Canada with ribbons of honor that no one would deny his right to equal citizenship.

"I do want to get back," Thomas said. "But first, Louise deserves a fine meal. Oats you said?"

Lance nodded. "Over there."

"Thank you." Thomas grabbed an empty feed bag and headed to the barrels.

"Any idea when?" Lance asked Jake.

Jake shook his head. Everyone knew that the Canadians were preparing to attack Vimy Ridge. Even the enemy troops knew. The only question was when.

To fool the enemy, General Byng had ordered extra heavy barrages of shelling to come without warning. The first few times, the enemy troops had prepared for a charge. But now they were exhausted after days of shelling. The enemy officers had difficulty getting their men in position because the men believed each new barrage was just a false alarm.

"And how is your leg?" Lance said. "Don't lie to me. I'm not your doctor."

"It could be better," Jake said. "It's the same with Thomas. Another week with the horses would be good. But any time we will get the word. So we can't wait. I'm sorry you can't join us."

Lance started to nod, then his eyes widened and he looked past Jake.

"What the . . ."

Jake turned.

He had never seen Thomas run so fast. His friend pushed past a few other soldiers and then dove into a man who was lifting a feed bag of oats to a horse farther down the line.

Both of them tumbled into a ball.

And within seconds, four soldiers stood above Thomas, their rifles pointed downward.

"Stop right there!" one of the soldiers yelled.

Jake began to sprint in his friend's direction. He didn't feel any pain in his leg. Only fear for his friend.

———•———

When Jake reached his friend, Thomas was still on the ground, with rifles pointed at him.

"Jake, take that horse by the halter," Thomas said. "Do not let her eat those oats. Look for nails."

Jake didn't ask why Thomas wanted him to do this. He had learned to trust his friend.

Jake took the horse by the halter and lifted her head away from the ground.

Tiny nails were scattered on the ground among the oats.

Jake turned to the soldiers. "Look at this. If the horse had eaten those oats, the nails would have torn apart her stomach."

One of the soldiers glanced at the nails on the ground. He lowered his rifle and picked up the feed bag that had fallen. He shook oats and more small nails out of the feed bag.

This soldier spoke to the others. "Let him stand. He was saving the horse."

As Thomas stood, he said to the man he had tackled, "I found nails in the barrel as I was getting oats for my horse. I did not know if you would listen in time if I yelled for you to stop feeding your horse. I am sorry. I saw no other way but to tackle you."

The man did not answer. He was shaking as he rolled onto his knees. Beads of sweat covered his face.

He stood.

He punched Thomas across the cheek.

Thomas rolled his head with the punch. He rubbed his cheek. "I take it then that you do not accept my apology."

"I could have stopped the war," the man said in a choked voice. "I could have stopped the war!"

The man dropped to his knees and tried to gather the nails on the ground. "Help me. Help me. I can't stand the noise anymore. We need to stop the horses from taking shells to the guns. If we kill all the horses, the war will stop. Help me. Help me."

The man was frantic. He began to sob.

Jake let out a long sigh of sympathy for the man. Obviously, killing all the horses would not stop the war, but this man just as obviously believed it. Jake suspected the poor man was shell-shocked. This happened to some soldiers after enduring the strain of constant battle.

Jake looked at the other soldiers. "Can you take him to a doctor and ask them to examine him? My friend and I will check the rest of the feed to make sure there are no more nails."

—•—

It took Jake and Thomas a full hour of walking through the muddy water in the maze of trenches to reach the Storming Normans platoon. By then, night had settled, but the wind had not, and it drove sleet over the top of the trenches.

The welcome from Lieutenant Norman was warm, however.

Not as warm as from Colonel Scruffington. The dog stayed in full salute for one minute, even after Thomas said "at ease."

"Good to see both of you," Lieutenant Norman said. "I know it's been a long day, but orders could come at any time for the attack. Now that you are back we need you to memorize your portion of the map."

This was not a surprise to Jake. It was common knowledge among all the soldiers that each division leader had a thick binder with complete plans of the attack. This had been broken into many small pieces, so that every section of six to nine soldiers had their own detailed map. The maps were marked with exactly what the small group needed to accomplish.

It made Jake feel like he was trusted by the commanding officers and that they felt he was smart enough to do what needed to be done.

He remembered what Major McNaughton had passed along from General Byng just before giving them medals of honor. *I want soldiers with the discipline of a well-trained pack of hounds. Soldiers who will find their own holes through the hedges. I'm not going to tell them where those holes are or how to get through them. I want soldiers who can find those holes themselves and get through those holes their own way. Soldiers who will never lose sight of the objective as they do it.*

Down in the trench, they were safe from the wind. They studied the maps by candlelight.

"We're going to be able to do this," Thomas said. "I can feel it in my bones. All four of our Canadian divisions together for the first time? We're going to do what everyone else thinks can't be done."

Jake felt that pride too. The British had failed to take Vimy Ridge. The French had failed to take Vimy Ridge. But he and the rest of the platoon had spent weeks and weeks training for this. They would fight for Canada. More importantly, they would fight for each other. Jake was glad to be back, even though he knew it would be dangerous.

Lieutenant Norman stopped by again.

Colonel Scruffington stood with his shoulder pressed to Thomas's knee as if he was afraid Thomas might go away again. That made Jake sad. Thomas *was* about to go away: into battle.

"Are you both good with what you need to do when we go? You have the instructions and map memorized?"

Jake and Thomas nodded.

"Good," Lieutenant Norman said. "When we get the call to go, I won't have time to say much except do your best. So now is when I have to remind you of the most critical part of the attack. And this comes directly from General Byng, so I need you to listen as if your lives depend on it. Because your lives do depend on this. Ready?"

Jake and Thomas nodded again.

Lieutenant Norman said, "The barrage of shells is going to be like a moving curtain in front of you. This curtain is going to be your protection from the enemy. It means when you go over the trenches, you have to be like a railroad train. Exactly to the second. If you move too quickly, you'll run into that curtain of explosives, and you'll be dead. If you move too slowly, the enemy will recover before you can pounce on them in the trenches. That's why we taught you the Vimy Glide. Tell me you both understand."

Jake and Thomas nodded for the third time.

"Not good enough," Lieutenant Norman said. "You need to tell me you understand. Each of you."

"I understand," Thomas said.

"I understand," Jake echoed.

"Good then," Lieutenant Norman said. "You need to do one last thing before sleep. Write your letters to your loved ones and hand them to me. I'll pass them down the line for safekeeping."

Jake knew exactly what that meant. He leaned over and scratched Colonel Scruffington's head. Some of them might not make it home.

He was far less afraid of dying than he was of letting down his fellow soldiers. He wanted to be there for Thomas and Charlie and the others. Jake belonged to the platoon.

—•—

Louise belonged to the herd. Not just a herd of other creatures like herself. In the herd were the two-legged creatures that made soothing sounds as they patted her side and rubbed her nose.

Louise felt safe in the herd, even in the dark. Even when she was awake at a time that she normally slept.

There was wind and sleet as she plodded through mud. She felt the itch of her hide and it hurt to walk. Her belly was tight and she wished she could drop her head and find thick grass. She felt the tremendous weight on her back of the load that had just been placed by those two-legged creatures. But her pain mattered less than loyalty to the herd.

There had been one two-legged creature in particular who led her by the halter, and the soothing sounds that came from this creature were a particular rhythm that she enjoyed, but he was not with her anymore.

Someone else held her halter. Someone else guided her. Something about the smell of this creature's skin said that tonight there was an urgency to making sure the herd moved forward.

Louise could hear the sounds of hundreds of others in the herd, plodding forward in the dark in the mud.

She knew where they going. They had gone there many, many times before. They were going to the smell of the big iron and the smell of bitterness from loud sounds, where the load would be taken off her back. Then the creature beside her would lead her back to where they had started, and another load would go on her back.

It was strange to do this at night, but Louise was part of the herd. Louise felt safe in the herd. Louise felt loyalty to the herd.

Louise moved forward in the night.

———•———

The wind had picked up in the night, and the sleet had thickened. Jake and Thomas and Charlie stood in the trenches with the rest of the platoon, waiting for time to tick down to precisely 5:30 a.m.

An hour earlier, Lieutenant Norman had tapped on their shoulders, telling them it was the morning for the attack. Every Canadian soldier able to fight was ready. Every single soldier! Jake knew he would never forget the date: April 9, 1917.

Dawn for them did not come gradually.

To the second, at 5:30 a.m., the pitch-black night sky blossomed into a brightness so intense that Jake could have read a newspaper. A split second later came the sound that shook his entire body.

It was as if twenty locomotives had collided directly in front of him. He'd thought the previous seven days of shelling were loud, but this was as if the very earth had been struck by a meteor. Jake had a quick vision of the lines upon lines of packhorses that had served to move all those explosives from the trains to the artillery and realized that the shell-shocked soldier had been right. Without the packhorses, there would have been no attack.

At the first of the explosions, the Canadian trenches erupted with thousands upon thousands of soldiers and Jake scrambled forward with them.

There was no time to give in to any kind of terror. It was too loud to be afraid. It was too bright to be afraid. It was nearly impossible to even think.

But because of the weeks of training, Jake found that it was almost as if his body took control, and he found himself gliding forward with the exact rhythm of all those times under the stopwatch. One step every two seconds. No more. No less. One hundred yards every three minutes.

It was almost as bright as daylight. Just in front of him, a sheet of explosives came down, like someone behind him was shooting a stream of water over his head and he could almost reach out and touch the spray as the water landed.

Except this spray consisted of the largest artillery bursts ever fired in the history of all mankind. He glanced left and glanced right. There were clumps of soldiers as far as he could see, all marching with determination behind that protective sheet of explosives.

Few men were falling. The driving sleet was at their backs, making it even more difficult for the enemy to see what was happening behind the approaching barrage of explosions.

This barrage was overwhelming to the point of being super-natural. Despite the advantage of fighting from a trenched position, no army in the world would have been able to deal with the barrage. Their enemy could not shoot, not when it had to cope with the shaking of the earth, the thunder that vibrated their bodies and the massive explosions that crept closer and closer at the exact pace of one hundred yards every three minutes.

Jake concentrated on his pace. One step every two seconds. One step every two seconds. One step every two seconds.

The map that Lieutenant Norman had given him was etched in his mind. Jake knew where to go and what to do when he got there. Thomas and Charlie and the rest of the platoon were by his side. Today was the day.

One step every two seconds. Follow the curtain of explosives. One step every two seconds. The Vimy Glide.

They reached the enemy trench, and right at that moment, the barrage that had ripped apart those trenches stopped.

To his left and to his right, up and down a ridge that was nearly ten kilometers (6 mi.) long, soldiers like Jake and Thomas and Charlie cut their way past the barbed wire, swarmed machine gun posts, dropped into the trenches and chased down the enemy.

Vimy Ridge belonged to them.

BEHIND-THE-SCENES HEROES

THE INSPIRATION BEHIND

LOUISE THE PACKHORSE

One of the most crucial elements to taking Vimy Ridge was moving thousands of tons of armament.

For this reason, the packhorses were almost as important as the soldiers. Patiently and under horrible conditions, the animals steadily brought 42,500 kilograms (93,700 lb.) of ammunition to the front lines—every single day! During the buildup to the battle and the battle itself, the eventual total reached 38 million kilograms (84 million lb.).

For the entire Vimy Ridge operation, then, it took the equivalent of a line of dump trucks seventy kilometers (43 mi.) long to deliver what was needed. While the trucks of that era were capable of moving ammunition, the mud and the poor condition of the roads were too much of an obstacle. The packhorses were so vital that, without them, attacking Vimy Ridge would

have been as much a disaster for the Canadians as it had been during the previous failed attempts by the French and British. Since a healthy packhorse can carry about 20 percent of its body weight, a line of all the horses it would take to carry this load would stretch 1,340 kilometers (833 mi.), nearly the distance from Ottawa to the coast of Newfoundland.

SHELL SHOCK

Imagine the physical toll war would take: sleepless nights, fatigue, injuries. Now imagine the mental toll: intense and constant bombardment, noise, danger and the knowledge that you or your comrades could die at any moment—or be responsible for the death of a similar solider on the opposite side.

During World War One, some soldiers began to report symptoms typical of physical head injuries, including amnesia, headaches, dizziness, tremors and a high sensitivity to noise. Many of these soliders were unable to reason or sleep or walk or talk. This was puzzling at first, because the men had no physical wounds to the brain.

Eventually these symptoms were recognized as a mental illness brought on by the stress of combat. Called shell shock then, and later, in World War Two, combat stress reaction, the brains of the affected soldiers would do strange things to try and make sense of the horrors of war.

Soldiers showing symptoms were taken away from the front line as soon as possible. For short-term shell shock, a few days of rest were often considered enough of a cure and soldiers were sent back to the front. Other soldiers, however, never overcame the illness. Ten years after the war, 65,000 veterans were still in treatment for it, and nineteen British military hospitals were totally devoted to treating those cases. Although not all soldiers were diagnosed with shell shock, all soldiers left the war changed—the brutality of what they experienced and witnessed meant that no soldier escaped unscathed.

THE WEEK OF SUFFERING AND THE ROLLING BARRAGE

5:30 came and a great light lit the place, a light made up of innumerable flickering tongues, which appeared from the void and extended as far to the south as the eye could see, a light which rippled and lit the clouds in that moment of silence before the crash and thunder of the battle smote the senses. Then the Ridge in front was wreathed in flame as the shells burst, confining the Germans to their dugouts while our men advanced to the assault.

—Private Lewis Duncan to his aunt Sarah, April 17, 1917

In the last lead-up to the attack on Vimy Ridge, there were three important preparations taking place. First, General Byng made it his goal that every soldier knew the plan of attack. This way they would be able to continue to fight no matter what—even without the guidance of officers. They all knew the plans, just not when the attack would come.

The second major preparation was digging tunnels beneath the German lines. Soldiers set up explosives to be detonated when the attack first began, which took extensive mining operations and tunnel systems with tracks, piped water and lights.

With all this in place, there was still a final part to the strategy before the attack could begin: the armament brought in by packhorses.

Spread over the course of a week before the attack, the Canadians began a massive barrage of shelling on the German trenches. With the constant bombardment, the Germans could guess a major attack was coming, but they could not know for certain when. The shelling was also designed to keep the Germans from sleeping, and over the course of those seven days, more than one million shells bombarded Vimy Ridge. One million! This generated numerous false alarms on the Germans side, and the barrage ensured that the enemy soldiers were tired to the point of exhaustion even before the attack began.

It was such an effective ploy that the Germans have called this softening of their forces "The Week of Suffering."

The Vimy Ridge attack itself began at 5:30 a.m. on Easter Monday, April 9, 1917. At that precise moment, another barrage began, and 20,000 Canadian soldiers, each carrying up to 36 kilograms (80 lb.) of combined equipment, jumped out of the trenches into snow, sleet and machine gun fire.

As the soldiers crossed No Man's Land, they were protected by a rolling barrage, the reason that they had trained so long to perfect the Vimy Glide: directly in front of them, like a moving waterfall, the falling shells served as a screen and as protection.

THE BATTLE OF VIMY RIDGE

In those few minutes, I witnessed the birth of a nation.
—Brigadier-General A.E. Ross, following the war

While most of the battle was won on the first day, from the opening barrage on April 9, 1917, the battle for Vimy Ridge lasted until April 12, 1917. It was the first time that all four Canadian divisions battled together. Trained to improvise in pursuit of a well-established goal and to understand what was ahead of them, some individual soldiers were able to force surrender of groups of Germans in their well-protected trenches, while others single-handedly charged machine gun nests.

Military historians all agree that the infantry used a combination of incredible discipline and bravery to advance under heavy fire and in confusing, hectic conditions, even when their officers fell and were no longer able to issue commands.

It was a victory that came with a cost that will never be forgotten: 3,598 Canadians were killed and another 7,000 wounded.

In 1922, the French government gave Vimy Ridge and the land around it to Canada forever.

EPILOGUE

D ale Montague was the Indian agent on the reserve. He was
a large man with a large voice and a bushy blond beard
that he constantly scratched.

He sat behind his desk at the reserve office and said one
word. "No."

Thomas had expected it. He did not like to ask the agent
for permissions because the agent always seemed to take extra
pleasure in saying no to Thomas.

Thomas was there because of the third person in the office:
his grandfather, William Northstar.

"There is no reason that you should deny a travel pass to my
grandfather," Thomas said. "His sister does not have long to live.
My grandfather will return from Regina after the funeral."

Actually, Thomas thought, there was no reason at all that
his grandfather should even need a pass. Why did the Cree
need permission to leave the reserve? How could a basic freedom like travel be taken away from them?

Montague stood. This was how he liked to deal with people.
Using his size and voice. As if the power of being Indian agent
was not enough.

"No," Montague repeated. He scratched his beard. "And I
do not need to explain myself."

Colonel Scruffington growled. The dog had refused to leave
Thomas when the war was over, so Thomas had smuggled

him onto the train and onto the boat to Canada and taken him home. Colonel Scruffington still limped and still slept beside Thomas every night.

"You may not like me," Thomas said, "but that is no reason to punish my grandfather."

William Northstar's hair was fully gray. He stood as tall as Thomas but had begun to stoop just a little. They shared a house at the edge of the reserve on the farmland that Thomas used to raise cattle.

"I am judge and jury on this reserve," Montague said. "I make the decisions around here, no matter how many letters you send to Ottawa. When will you give that up? Nobody believes your word over mine. Everybody knows that Indians are liars."

Thomas reminded himself of the discipline he and the other soldiers had learned at Vimy Ridge. If he lost his temper, Montague could call in the police and have him arrested. He knew that was why Montague always tried to make him angry.

A shotgun was hanging from a rack on the wall. Montague walked to it and took it in both hands.

"Your dog growled at me," Montague said. "It is a dangerous animal and I am tired of it."

Montague pointed the shotgun at Colonel Scruffington.

Colonel Scruffington growled again.

Thomas stood directly over his dog, his legs on either side. Thomas said to the larger man. "Look in my eyes. Do you really want to pull the trigger? Because then you will have to shoot me too as the only way to stop me from breaking every finger on your hand."

"Are you threatening me?" Montague asked. "I can have you thrown in jail for that."

"He is protecting his dog," William Northstar said. "Just as I will protect my grandson."

"Get out of my office," Montague said. "All three of you. And if you leave the reserve without a pass, I will make sure you're arrested. A telephone call will reach Regina much faster than you can."

—·—

On a hot spring afternoon about a week later, Thomas and William Northstar walked along a straight road in Regina and looked for a building with the number nineteen.

"This is dizzying," William told Thomas. "So many houses that look so much the same in so many rows. I can only marvel at such a display. But where is the beauty in this? A river bed flows and curves, as do hills and flowers. There is nothing natural in how the white men assembled all of this."

"And yet," Thomas said, "you think the automobile is a wonderful invention."

"You can walk down the road after an automobile has passed by and not worry about where to step," William said. "This cannot be said for a horse. Before I pass from this earth, I would like to drive an automobile and wave at all my friends as I go by."

"You mean ride *in* an automobile," Thomas said. "Not drive. Please tell me that your ambition goes no further than being a passenger."

"Drive," William said firmly. "A magnificent automobile like the one that approaches us now."

This automobile slowed and stopped.

"This is why I do not want you to ever drive," Thomas said. "Your vision is terrible. That automobile belongs to the Regina Police."

A constable stepped out of the vehicle.

He was a man about Thomas's age, a very big man. As he walked toward them, Thomas realized he had seen the man before.

Thomas said, "Mark Lipton! It is good to see you! I did not know you had joined the police force."

"Thomas," Mark said. "It is good to see you and your grandfather, but I wish it were under different circumstances. There's a warrant out for your arrest. When it came in, I said that it must be wrong because I knew you from the platoon and you were a war hero and one of the best soldiers anyone could ask for. The warrant said you might try to visit the hospital, so they sent me to patrol this area to keep an eye out for you. My captain also said to tell you to take as much time as you would like with your visit. The hospital is around the next corner. After you are finished, I will drive you where you need to go."

Thomas stared at Mark. "I do not understand."

"Many of us think the pass system is unfair," Mark said. "We do our best not to enforce it."

"Neither is it fair that I have to get permission from an Indian agent to sell wheat or cattle or buy farm equipment," Thomas said. "And neither is it fair that I cannot sell my own land without permission. Neither is it fair that I cannot be a citizen in my own country after I fought alongside men like you to protect it."

"I agree with all of that," Mark said.

"Except that now you will have to break the law to help a friend. And you as a policeman must hide me away from the law you serve because I am helping my grandfather visit his dying sister. Is that not wrong as well? Should not the law be changed instead of ignored or broken?"

"Are you saying that I should arrest you?" Mark asked, scratching his head.

"If I am living life as a prisoner in my own country, what

difference does it make if I am prisoner on my farm or in a jail cell? Maybe in a jail cell, I can get someone in the government to listen to me."

Mark looked closely at Thomas. "I think I understand . . . You knew by leaving the reserve without a pass that the agent put out a warrant. You *wanted* to get arrested."

"I knew my grandfather needed to see his sister and needed my help to travel," Thomas said. "As for the rest, I have been angry for many years. Why was I an equal during the war when we faced death but not after the war on my own land? It is not that I am here to fight. It is that I do not know what else to do. If you are kind, you will arrest us after my grandfather spends time with his sister."

William said to Mark Lipton, "And perhaps I can share a jail cell with my grandson? He has yet to beat me in chess but never tires of trying. It is an amusing way to pass time."

—•—

Just before stepping out of the police station, Willam said to Thomas. "There is no need to be glum. It was only a week in jail. How could you expect to win a chess game against me in that short amount of time?"

Thomas did not smile. "If that was all I needed to worry about, I would be a happy man. I do not like this, not knowing why we are suddenly free to go."

They walked out of the building just as a nearby church bell chimed noon. Thomas was glad it was a cloudy day. After his time in the jail cell, daylight seemed too bright as it was.

The city street in front of them was wide and filled with traffic. But Thomas only noticed the shiny new automobile parked directly in front of the police station.

"It is as I feared," Thomas said to his grandfather. "My two friends Jake and Charlie."

They were already stepping out of the car. Charlie wore a fine suit. Jake had on a working man's clothes. Both had big grins.

Thomas wanted to smile back, but set his lips straight and his expression stern.

"Hello, Charlie," Thomas said. "Hello, Jake. This is my grandfather, William Northstar."

"It is nice to meet you," William said. "And that is a fine automobile. A very fine automobile."

"Why are you here?" Thomas asked Charlie and Jake. He remained on the sidewalk and people had to move around them.

"Train from Toronto," Charlie said. "Jake jumped aboard in Winnipeg. A family friend met us at the train station here and loaned us this Packard. Nice city, this Regina. Fifty thousand people already. I'll have to report back to my father that we seriously need to invest money in a place growing this fast."

"That is not what I meant and you know it," Thomas said. "Why are you here?"

"You had already spent too much time in jail," Jake said. "It was time to get you out. We talked to a judge and paid your bail."

"I was afraid that would be your answer. This does not make me happy."

Jake grinned at William. "It must wear you out when he gets all high and mighty and angry about things."

"Very much," William answered, "but he is family, so I must accept it. Did I mention that is a very fine automobile? I do not suppose there is a chance that one of you two fine young men could teach me to drive it?"

"Grandfather," Thomas said, "my friends did not come to visit and take us for an automobile ride. They came to rescue me, even if I did not ask for it."

"It is what friends do, Thomas," William said. "Look at this automobile. A Packard? Magnificent."

"It is my fight," Thomas told William. "It is not their fight."

Thomas looked at Charlie. "After the war, the SPCA did everything possible to save all the animals who helped soldiers. I am very glad for that. I am not glad that those animals receive better treatment and sympathy than those of us who have had to return to reserves where the government forgets that we stood shoulder to shoulder with the rest of the country's soldiers during the Great War."

"I am not happy about that either," Charlie said.

"Neither am I," Jake said. "Nor am I happy that not once did you write to me or Charlie about what you were facing. We are brothers. Didn't you say that? One blood. One nation."

"I have learned since that our government acts as if it is two bloods and two nations. You are both like brothers to me, but I do not want your help."

Charlie said, "Thomas, you know I'm from the city. If the two of us were alone in the middle of the Prairies, I would gladly ask you to shoot game for me and help me build a shelter. Just as I would gladly help you find your way around the city. Right or wrong, we live in two different worlds. Much as I wish the two of us together could change the system, I fear it will take another generation for that. In the meantime, let me help you in my world and—"

"Yes," Thomas interrupted, "I would shoot game for you if you were starving or injured. Until then, I would let you go hungry for a long time until you learned to hunt for yourself and relied on your own strength. That is what a friend and brother would do. I will not permit you to coddle me into weakness. You have rescued me from jail. So what? I still live in prison on my reserve."

Thomas spoke to William. "Come on, Grandfather. We need to return to our cell and finish our chess game. You were very lucky, you know. I was just about to beat you before the lawyer told us we were free to go."

"Thomas," Jake said. "Charlie and I didn't come here to rescue you. We came here because you had already rescued yourself. I think you should listen to what we have to say."

William spoke to Jake. "Perhaps as we listen, we can go for a ride around the city in this fine automobile? Somewhere along the way, I am sure, there will be a place where you can teach me how to drive."

—•—

Thomas stepped into the Indian agent office. Dale Montague looked up from behind his desk.

"You are supposed to be in jail in Regina," Montague said. He scratched his beard. Thomas suspected fleas.

"Before I left the reserve," Thomas said, "I had a serious conversation with my dog. I told him that he was to make sure that you never saw him. I have already heard that while I was gone you went hunting for him nearly every day and failed to find him. It is a wonderful joke on the reserve. The agent who cannot find an old dog. Some also say that is not a surprise, since they doubt you can find your buttocks with your own hands."

"How dare you?" Montague sputtered as he stood up. "You will not be laughing when you find yourself back in jail again."

The door opened. Colonel Scruffington walked inside and growled at Montague.

Then Jake walked in. Thomas remained standing. Jake sat in a chair at the side of the office, and Colonel Scruffington sat next to him.

"Who are you?" Montague asked Jake.

Jake just stared at Montague until the agent looked away.

Charlie opened the door and stood in the doorway, looking imposing in his expensive dark suit.

Montague stared at Charlie, and then gaped at what he saw outside the door. "Is that William Northstar sitting behind the wheel of a Packard?"

"It is," Jake told Montague. "He forgot to mention that he is blind in one eye. It explains a lot about his driving."

Charlie closed the door.

"I suppose that's the shotgun?" Charlie asked Thomas, pointing at where it rested on its rack.

"You suppose that is what shotgun?" Montague asked. "Who are you and—"

"It's come to my attention that you used a shotgun to threaten a distinguished war veteran," Charlie said. "Is that the shotgun?"

"I never pointed it at Thomas," Montague said. "If he told you that, he's a liar. Like the rest of his people. You can't trust anything they—"

"Not that war veteran," Jake said. "This war veteran."

Jake reached over and scratched Colonel Scruffington's head.

"This is ridiculous," Montague said. He glared at Charlie. "Who are you?"

"Charlie Austin." Charlie remained standing, arms crossed.

"What business is it of yours if I shoot a mangy old Indian dog?" Montague asked. "You could be from the Austin family of Toronto and I wouldn't . . ."

Charlie smiled as Montague grew quiet.

"Yes," Charlie said. "I'm aware you're from Toronto. I have the file with most of your employment history."

Montague drew a breath. "Well, in Toronto you might be in the know of those who run the city, but here—"

"The years since the war have been good to me," Charlie said. "I learned a lot in my platoon, and it's served me well. At this point, my 'in the know' goes beyond those who run the city."

"Province then," Montague said. "But here—"

Charlie pointed upward.

The agent looked at the ceiling.

"He means in the know of those higher than the province," Jake whispered.

"Unless the prime minister himself sent you," Montague said, "you have no powers here. I am justice and jury on this reserve, and you can't do a thing about it. So I don't care why you're here. You and your friend might as well turn around. Try not to get horse manure on those fancy shoes of yours. This isn't Toronto, and nobody here is going to roll out the red carpet for you."

"I have managed to control my temper around you since the day you stepped on this reserve," Thomas said. "But if you do not treat my friend with respect, this will become the day when I do something I will regret. I promise you'll regret it more than I will."

"Your *friends*." Montague sneered. "All these years on the reserve, you have not once said that you know Charlie Austin."

"Don't forget me," Jake said. "There are two of us here."

"Thomas saved my life," Charlie said. "And we are here because of the letters that Thomas has been sending over the years since the war."

Montague rolled his eyes. "Oh yes. Those stupid letters.

Citizenship for those Indians who fought. Equal benefits for Indian veterans. He is tireless in his complaints."

Montague turned to Thomas. "I guess you've finally realized that you Indians can't make it in our world without help. And even then, these friends won't be able to do a thing for you, Austin family or not. So here's my advice to you, Charlie Austin and . . ."

"Jake," Jake said. "Jake York. Easy name to remember."

"I won't need to," Montague answered. "Here's my advice to both of you: don't let the door hit you on the way out. Thomas Northstar does not have my permission to leave with you. I will not sign his pass. He cannot travel without it."

"You're wrong about something," Charlie said. "Although I am proud Thomas Northstar calls me a friend, I am not here as his friend."

"Same goes for me," Jake said.

"So about those letters," Charlie said. "A few months ago, a colleague of mine named Stuart in Indian Affairs thought that Thomas's name seemed familiar. Eventually Stu remembered the many occasions I had talked about my good friend and Cree warrior Thomas Northstar. Because of that, when Thomas was arrested in Regina, Stu made sure it came to my attention and I took the first train there."

Charlie gave Montague a cold smile. "But you are right about something else, too."

Jake said, "You mean the part where he said unless the prime minister himself sent you?"

"Jake, don't exaggerate," Charlie said. "The prime minister himself did not send me. Matters like this are handled by Indian Affairs. Please be clearer."

"Apologies," Jake said to Montague. "Indian Affairs sent Charlie because they've recommended to the prime minister that Thomas's complaints be investigated and the issues dealt with. But as the prime minister is good friends with the Austin family, he is naturally interested in this matter."

"The prime minister," the agent said in a dull voice of slow comprehension.

"He arrived at our Ottawa estate one day for lunch," Charlie said. "You remember it, right, Thomas?"

"On the Rideau River, just down from Parliament," Thomas said. "Great place to rest on our way back from France. Remember how the Colonel here managed to grab a roasted chicken from the kitchen and had to be chased down by one of your maids?"

"The prime minister," Montague repeated.

"Yes," Charlie said. "During lunch, he specifically brought up the subject of Thomas Northstar and these complaints. He said he agreed with Indian Affairs and wondered, since I was friends with Thomas, whether I'd be interested in making a visit to deliver a letter in person in regards to the complaints."

"It's no different than plenty other reserves," Montague said. "You try dealing with—"

"Wrong again," Jake said. "Plenty other reserves have fair agents who try to do the right thing even with a bad system. Who don't insist on using passes to control people. Who allow farmland to be bought and sold. Who allow produce to be bought and sold. Who don't feel they have the right to hunt down animals that belong to those living on the reserve. You really wanted to shoot Colonel Scruffington, didn't you? A veteran. Shame on you."

"Indian Affairs agrees with Jake here," Charlie said. "Plenty of fair agents out there. They've decided it's time this reserve gets a fair agent too."

Thomas handed Montague a letter. "This is from Indian Affairs. Near the end, you will find a portion of special interest to me. The portion that states Jake York has been given duties as temporary agent until a replacement reaches us."

Montague read the letter twice and finally managed to say, "I've been discharged."

Charlie said, "Don't take a single thing as you go. Everything belongs to Indian Affairs."

"Including the shotgun," Jake said. "Now that I'm a temporary agent, it's my responsibility."

Jake stepped to the wall and took down the shotgun. He made sure it wasn't loaded. Then he put the end of the barrel on the floor and held the stock. He stepped on it and snapped the shotgun barrel from the wood stock.

Jake kicked the pieces aside, sat in the agent's chair and put his feet up on the desk and crossed his hands behind his neck. He said to Montague, "Mind if I offer you some advice now that you are unemployed?"

"What's that?" Montague asked.

Jake said, "Don't let the door hit you on your way out."

Colonel Scruffington followed Montague to the door.

"Scruff," Thomas said. "Stay away. I don't want you to get fleas."

The Colonel growled one last time at Montague as he stepped outside, the dazed look on his face made worse by the image of a smiling William Northstar behind the steering wheel of a new Packard.

As Montague walked down the road, William Northstar cheerfully honked the horn.

FIRST NATIONS SOLDIERS AND FRANCIS PEGAHMAGABOW

The war proved that the fighting spirit of my tribe was not squelched through reservation life. When duty called, we were there, and when we were called forth to fight for the cause of civilization, our people showed all the bravery of our warriors of old.
—Mike Mountain Horse, First World War veteran

Many First Nations soldiers served as platoon leaders and combat instructors; at least fifty have been decorated for bravery in battle.

Because of this, many of the First Nations soldiers hoped that on their return to Canada they would get recognition and improved living conditions because of their achievements and sacrifices during the war. While they did receive some benefits after the war, it was still not equal to the benefits given to other veterans.

Indeed, on September 1, 1919, the Six Nations veterans sent a letter to the deputy superintendent general of Indian Affairs in Ottawa that began as follows:

"Sir, we the undersigned, members of the Six Nations Indians, loyal soldiers of His Majesty The King, of the Township of Tuscarora in the county of Brant do most humbly implore and petition you Sir to hearken and consider our cry for deliverance from our present system of government . . . and we hope and pray that, the 'Canada' for which our friends and comrades fought and died, the same 'Canada,' we fought and gladly suffered for, may see fit to grant us this change."

The most decorated First Nations soldier in World War One was Francis Pegahmagabow. Shortly after arriving in France, Pegahmagabow fought in the Second Battle of Ypres, where he faced the chlorine gas that the Germans unleashed for the first time in war history. Next, at the Battle of Somme, he was wounded in the left leg, but returned to action. In a later battle, by then a corporal, he guided lost reinforcements to their place along the line. After that, during the Battle of the Scarpe, with his company almost out of ammunition, he faced machine gun and rifle fire to go into No Man's Land and return with enough ammunition for his company to fight off the enemy.

Upon his return to Canada, he actively tried to make political change, based in part on his dislike of his Indian agent, and tried to free his people from "white slavery." In 2016 on National Aboriginal Day, his memory was honored with a life-sized bronze monument unveiled in Parry Sound, Ontario.

Many World War One First Nations veterans were involved in similar attempts for political change. Their travel experiences had given them a wider perspective on their home situations, and they felt that since they had earned the respect of the soldiers beside them in the trenches, they deserved the same rights as veterans back in Canada.

So many First Nations chiefs sent letters to the Department of Indian Affairs that, in 1933, this department changed its policy and did not allow chiefs to correspond with the department directly anymore. Instead, the new policy forced them to work through their Indian agents. Given that many of the letters addressed complaints *about* Indian agents, it reduced the power of First Nations chiefs.

PASS SYSTEM

Because of the Northwest Rebellion led by Louis Riel, members of the Canadian government worried that First Nations people would leave their reserves to join the fight. And even though the act of requiring passes for First Nations to travel violated treaty rights, the system was put into place.

This system required that before a First Nations person could travel—regardless of the reason—the local Indian agent had to sign a permission slip issued by the Department of Indian Affairs. Parents were denied the chance to visit their children at residential schools, children couldn't leave to visit elderly parents, and siblings might go years without seeing each other. The North West Mounted Police protested the system back in

1893, but they were overruled by the Department of Indian Affairs, even though the department head acknowledged the pass system was not grounded in law.

It was a system that lasted well past World War One. Leona Blondeau, from the George Gordon Reserve in Saskatchewan—where Thomas Northstar from the fictional story returns after the war—remembers that as a child, she needed to get permission to leave the reserve to travel by wagon to the closest town, Punnichy, even if all they were doing was going to get ice cream.

Leona was eight years old when the federal policy officially ended in 1941, but she recalls restrictions still lasting for years past that.

"We never went anywhere," she told a reporter. "We stayed on the reserve. We were very segregated. . . . It was the way life was, I thought. I didn't realize it wasn't the right thing to do."

First Nations World War One veterans, like all First Nations peoples across Canada, were not permitted to buy and sell land, or even produce, without permission from an Indian agent.

It was not until 1956, thirty-eight years after the war, that First Nations men and women were granted citizenship as Canadians.

WHEN THE GUNS FELL SILENT

The French forest north of Paris was made of beech trees and oak trees, a forest wide enough that it would take a day's walk to cross from one end to another. Here was quiet and shade, well away from the mortars and shelling of the Great War. And here, early in November, a secret meeting took place in a private rail car parked on a siding where tracks cut through the forest.

Those inside the train had arrived from Germany, and the location and secrecy were chosen to give them privacy from journalists and protection from any locals who might want to take revenge for the damage of the Great War.

Those inside the train were presented with a list of demands to end the war, and they were given seventy-two hours to sign. They had little choice. The Battle of Vimy Ridge, barely a year and a half earlier, had been one of a series of Allied victories that made winning the war inevitable, especially after the United States joined the war in 1917.

In that forest, at 5:00 a.m. Paris time, on November 11, 1918, those inside the rail car agreed to the terms of a cease-fire—known as an armistice—and signed a declaration that all fighting on land and air would stop within six hours.

On that same morning, 190 kilometers (120 mi.) to the north, Private George Lawrence Price was part of a force advancing into a small village in Belgium, determined to help stop a machine gunner who had fired on their troops during the crossing of a canal. He served with the "A" Company of the 28th Battalion of the Canadian Expeditionary Force. At 10:58 a.m., he was shot by a sniper.

Two minutes later, at the 11th hour on the 11th day of the 11th month of 1918, all shooting stopped. The guns were finally silent. After fifty-two months of horrendous fighting, the Great War was over. George Lawrence Price, age 25, was the final Canadian soldier to give up his life in the Great War.

This ceasefire remained in place until the Treaty of Versailles officially ended World War One. It was signed on June 28, 1919, exactly five years to the day after the assassination of Archduke Franz Ferdinand had begun the chain of events leading to the war.

On November 11, 1919, King George V hosted the first official Armistice Day events on the grounds of Buckingham Palace. This led to November 11 becoming Remembrance Day in many countries across the world, a day set aside to honor and acknowledge the sacrifices made by military and families during war, conflict and peace.

ACKNOWLEDGMENTS

Thank you to George Gordon First Nation Chief and Council for help with background and research. Thank you, too, for allowing me to include photos of George Gordon war veterans in the video documentary, which can be found at www.thebattleof vimyridge.com. Thanks so much to Samantha Swenson at Tundra Books for brilliant advice, much patience and a sense of humor that made working together on the project a lot of fun. And also thanks to Amy Tompkins at Transatlantic Agency; it's a great partnership.

SOURCES

While the following list shows the books used for research, I found two books in particular to be very useful in giving a sense of what it was like in the trenches for Canadian soldiers in World War One: *Over the Top* by Arthur Guy Empey and *Vimy* by Pierre Burton. *Over the Top* is an excellent informal portrayal of a soldier's daily life, and *Vimy* gives an amazing perspective on the significance of the Canadian victory at Vimy Ridge.

SELECTED BIBLIOGRAPHY

BOOKS

Baynes, Ernest Harold. *Animal Heroes of the Great War.* London: Albion Press, 2016.

Boyden, Joseph. *Three Day Road.* Toronto: Penguin Books, 2006.

Brewster, Hugh. *At Vimy Ridge: Canada's Greatest World War I Victory.* Markham, ON: Scholastic Canada, 2007.

Bulanda, Susan. *Soldiers in Fur and Feathers: The Animals That Served in World War I—Allied Forces.* Crawford, CO: Alpine Publications, 2013.

Burton, Pierre. *Vimy.* Toronto: McClelland & Stewart, 1986.

Cooper, Jilly. *Animals in War: Valiant Horses, Courageous Dogs, and Other Unsung Animal Heroes.* London: Corgi, 1984.

Empey, Arthur Guy. *Over the Top.* New York: G.P. Putnam's Sons, The Knickerbocker Press, 1917.

Granatstein, J.L. *The Greatest Victory: Canada's One Hundred Days.* Oxford: Oxford University Press, 2014.

Hayes, Adrian. *Pegahmagabow: Life-Long Warrior.* Toronto: Blue Butterfly, 2009.

Jenkins, Ryan. *World War 1: Soldier Stories—The Untold Soldier Stories on the Battlefields of WWI.* Success First Publishing, 2015.

Le Chêne, Evelyn. *Silent Heroes: The Bravery and Devotion of Animals in War.* London: Souvenir Press, 1994.

Story, Neil R. *Animals in the First World War.* Oxford: Shire Publications, 2014.

Winegard, Timothy C. *For King and Kanata: Canadian Indians and the First World War.* Winnipeg: University of Manitoba Press, 2012.

WEBSITE RESOURCES

For readers who would like to learn more about the Canadian Expeditionary Force in World War One, please visit this website: www.thebattleofvimyridge.com. You will find direct links to helpful websites about the Canadian forces in World War One, as well as links to articles and stories from the research behind *Innocent Heroes* and a teacher's guide available for download, with a glossary and terms.

PHOTOS

Every reasonable effort has been made to trace ownership of, and give credit to, copyrighted material.

LITTLE ABIGAIL

PAGE 1 (PIGEON)
All-silhouettes.com

PAGE 14
Cher Ami
www.atlasobscura.com/places/cher-ami (public domain)

PAGE 15
A man in British army uniform attaches a message to a carrier pigeon ready to fly.

National Library of Scotland, photographer David McLellan
http://digital.nls.uk/74548774
Used under the Creative Commons Attribution 4.0 International License

PAGE 16
Five horse-drawn mobile pigeon lofts parked around the perimeter of a small field. A soldier feeds the pigeons on the roof.

National Library of Scotland, photographer David McLellan
http://digital.nls.uk/74548776
Used under the Creative Commons Attribution 4.0 International License

PAGE 17
Two soldiers on motorbikes with wicker baskets strapped to their backs to carry pigeons.

National Library of Scotland, photographer David McLellan
http://digital.nls.uk/74548780
Used under the Creative Commons Attribution 4.0 International License

BOOMER

PAGE 19 (CAT)
Designed by Freepik.com

PAGE 35 (LEFT)
Togo, the mascot of the British battleship *Dreadnought*

Photo credit: © IWM
Licensed from the Imperial War Museums First World War Agency Collection

PAGE 35 (RIGHT)
A soldier in his shirtsleeves leans over a makeshift tub filled with water. Existing in the squalor of the trenches, soldiers rarely if ever had the opportunity to wash or change clothes. Unsuccessful attempts were occasionally made to kill off lice and other parasites by boiling uniforms in large vats of water.

National Library of Scotland, photographer John Warwick Brooke
http://digital.nls.uk/74547804
Used under the Creative Commons Attribution 4.0 International License

PAGE 36
Allied troops occupy a German trench.

National Library of Scotland, photographer John Warwick Brooke
http://digital.nls.uk/74548256
Used under the Creative Commons Attribution 4.0 International License

PAGE 37 (LEFT)
Soldiers build a dugout in the supporting reserve lines. Underground dugouts like these were used by officers for planning attacks, while soldiers used them for eating and resting.

National Library of Scotland, photographer John Warwick Brooke
http://digital.nls.uk/74547964
Used under the Creative Commons Attribution 4.0 International License

PAGE 37 (RIGHT)
Remains of a captured German trench after heavy artillery fire. The entrance to a tunnel gives some idea of the labyrinthine network of tunnels and trenches that formed the front line defenses on the Western Front.

PAGE 38

Stripped down to their shirts and braces, two British soldiers use a can of water to catch up on their washing.

COAL DUST

PAGE 41 (HORSE)

PAGE 59 (LEFT)

A group of cavalrymen

PAGE 59 (RIGHT)

Gas mask drill for horses

PAGE 60

Two British soldiers ride a team of packhorses through a deep stream. After it had been repeatedly proven that cavalry attacks had no place on the Western Front, many cavalry horses joined the packhorses and mules that were used to carry supplies.

TOMATO

PAGE 61 (DOG)
Designed by Freepik.com

PAGE 77
A dog with a gas mask. This dog was employed by a sanitary corps in locating wounded soldiers.

Photo by Francis Whiting Halsey
Public Domain: first published in the USA before 1923.

PAGE 78
Three men in a trench wearing gas masks.

National Library of Scotland, photographer John Warwick Brooke
http://digital.nls.uk/74547760
Used under the Creative Commons Attribution 4.0 International License

PAGE 79 (LEFT)
A dog-handler reads a message brought by a messenger dog, in France during World War One. The message would have been rolled up inside a waterproof container attached to the dog's collar.

National Library of Scotland, photographer Tom Aitken
http://digital.nls.uk/74549024
Used under the Creative Commons Attribution 4.0 International License

PAGE 79 (RIGHT)
British messenger dogs with their handler. Messenger dogs were based in sectional kennels near the front lines. On average, each sectional kennel had forty-eight dogs and sixteen handlers, a ratio that indicates how important the dogs' work was at the front.

National Library of Scotland, photographer Tom Aitken
http://digital.nls.uk/74549184
Used under the Creative Commons Attribution 4.0 International License

PAGE 80
Messenger dogs and their handlers marching to the front. In addition to carrying messages, these dogs probably performed a wide range of important tasks, including sentry duty, acting as decoys, ambulance duties and killing vermin.

LEO

PAGE 81 (BIG CAT SILHOUETTE)

PAGE 98

A soldier in a shallow trench with his pet dog.

PAGE 99

A man and a monkey stand next to a captured German trench mortar.

PAGE 100

R.A.F. Squadron's fox mascot in France during World War One.

PAGE 101

A triumphant dog sits atop a gun surrounded by gunners. Proudly perched on top of what looks like a howitzer, this pet dog was the regimental mascot of the artillery gunners also gathered around the gun.

CHARLIE

PAGE 103 (DONKEY)
Momentbloom / Vecteezy.com

PAGE 118
A line of mules carries ammunition for field artillery. Each animal has a pair of panniers, loaded with eight rounds of what appear to be eight-kilogram (18 lb.) shells for a field gun.

National Library of Scotland
http://digital.nls.uk/74549588
Used under the Creative Commons Attribution 4.0 International License

PAGE 119
A soldier and his mule at the Western Front.

National Library of Scotland
http://digital.nls.uk/74549584
Used under the Creative Commons Attribution 4.0 International License

PAGE 120
A mule stuck in a shell hole. This photograph shows French soldiers trying to pull an exhausted mule out of the mud of a shell hole. A second mule has been rescued and is standing to the left.

National Library of Scotland
http://digital.nls.uk/74549306
Used under the Creative Commons Attribution 4.0 International License

PAGE 121
Vickers machine gun crew

National Library of Scotland
http://digital.nls.uk/74549554
Used under the Creative Commons Attribution 4.0 International License

PAGE 123
A long line of soldiers and pack mules moves across a war-torn landscape.

National Library of Scotland, photographer John Warwick Brooke
http://digital.nls.uk/74547898
Used under the Creative Commons Attribution 4.0 International License

BISCOTTE

PAGE 125 (DOG)
Designed by Freepik.com

PAGE 141 (LEFT)
A bandaged dog that worked in the front line trenches, in France, during World War One. With bandages on all four paws, this dog—called Paddy—carried out a range of hazardous duties in a front line trench, despite the shellfire and poison gas.

National Library of Scotland, photographer Tom Aitken
http://digital.nls.uk/74549018
Used under the Creative Commons Attribution 4.0 International License

PAGE 141 (RIGHT)
Dog rescues the wounded

Wellcome Library, London
Collection: Wellcome Images "image_innopac_id" L0009138
Copyrighted work available under Creative Commons Attribution only licence CC BY 4.0

PAGE 142
Soldiers returning to trenches after a raid.

National Library of Scotland, photographer John Warwick Brooke
http://digital.nls.uk/74547530
Used under the Creative Commons Attribution 4.0 International License

LOUISE

PAGE 145 (PACKHORSE)
Mulpo_com / VectorOpenStock.com

PAGE 161 (LEFT)
A group of soldiers and horses

National Library of Scotland, photographer David McLellan
http://digital.nls.uk/74548672
Used under the Creative Commons Attribution 4.0 International License

PAGE 161 (RIGHT)

Packhorses transporting ammunition.

This image is available from Library and Archives Canada under the reproduction reference number PA-001231 and under the MIKAN ID number 3194763
Public Domain

PAGE 163 (LEFT)

Soldiers struggle to pull a big gun through mud. The gun has been placed on a track created for a light railway. A makeshift tread has been fitted to the wheels of the gun in an attempt to aid its movement through the mud.

National Library of Scotland, photographer Ernest Brooks
http://digital.nls.uk/74546544
Used under the Creative Commons Attribution 4.0 International License

PAGE 163 (RIGHT)

Two soldiers lifting a section of duckboard onto a packhorse.

National Library of Scotland, photographer John Warwick Brooke
http://digital.nls.uk/74547250
Used under the Creative Commons Attribution 4.0 International License

PAGE 164

A Canadian battalion goes "over the top" during World War One.

National Library of Scotland, photographer John Warwick Brooke
http://digital.nls.uk/74545832
Used under the Creative Commons Attribution 4.0 International License

EPILOGUE

PAGE 182

An example of a permission slip: Pat Grasshopper's pass to leave the reserve, Sarcee Indian Agency (Tsuu T'ina), southern Alberta.

Credit: Glenbow Archives, M-1837-22b

PAGE 183

Thomas McNab: First Nations soldier, George Gordon Reserve, Saskatchewan

Thank you to George Gordon First Nation Chief and Council for permission to use this photo.

INDEX